God of the Hinge

God of the Hinge:
Sojourns in Cloud Cuckoo Land

Elizabeth Pool and Eleanor West

Augusta

God of the Hinge: Sojourns in Cloud Cuckoo Land
By Elizabeth Pool and Eleanor West
A Harbor House Book/2006

For information address:
HARBOR HOUSE
111 TENTH ST.
AUGUSTA, GA 30901

Library of Congress Cataloging-in-Publication Data

Pool, Elizabeth.

God of the hinge : sojourns in Cloud Cuckoo Land / by Elizabeth Pool & Eleanor West.

p. cm.

ISBN 1-891799-32-0

1. Travel--Miscellanea. 2. Travelers--Anecdotes. I. West, Eleanor. II. Title.

G465.P66 2005

910.4--dc22

2005022892

Printed in the United States of America

10 9 8 7 6 5 4 3 2 1

For H, because our adventure means *something. We can discern footprints if we look down, pathways if we look ahead, starlight, moonlight and odd-shaped rainbows if we look up. We haven't become missionaries and we certainly aren't busy developing any kind of doctrine. We have, however, been brought to see a lot of stuff we* don't *think, stuff that gets in the way of shimmering truths almost lost but still lurking.*

PROLOGUE

RUSTY

Dear Melanie, eldest of the grands and greats:

This is the story of an adventure in which your grandmother and your great-aunt have been entangled for more than 60 years. It tells of a strange pursuit that grew into an affair involving not a pair but a trio.

We never sought this adventure. We just found ourselves in it, the way you find yourself taking part in a dream, knowing nothing about the script. But it wasn't and isn't a dream, and we feel we must get it all down while there is still time.

The overture was set in a train station. Like all big city stations in the old days, the New York Grand Central was a palace with lots of gold and marble and tiers of glass. The imperious locomotives that drew the trains blew long, echoing hoots as they sped across the country, coast to coast and border to border. There were, of course, cars and trucks and buses, but many, many fewer than today. The train was king. All lesser vehicles traveling the highways and byways were simply his subjects.

The setting where we met was regal, as it had to be. The year was 1935. I see myself: a tall, thin, serious figure, standing on a platform waiting for the approach of a shining monster. My hair, very thick and reddish, is largely covered by a hat. No lady goes out in the city without hat and gloves and I am most certainly a lady, as my mother has been reminding me since adolescence. I have now been married for a year, and she is still reminding me.

There is a shriek of brakes. Steam bursts from the train. I choke. I am blinded. I open my eyes and there she is, walking straight toward me, though we have never met. She is small, sparkly and what I can see of her hair (because of course she too is wearing a hat) is very blonde.

She is engaged to marry my brother. The train has brought her halfway across the country to meet her future in-laws, who are formal people and wait to greet her in a formal establishment.

Nothing could be easier than collecting the luggage, finding a taxi and proceeding to the all-important lunch. We collect the luggage, we find a taxi, but we do not proceed to lunch. We go to a dress shop, haul the suitcases out of the taxi and stack them by the door, to the dismay of the polished shop owner.

Do we need dresses? Not particularly. Will we be late for lunch? Yes. Will we be in trouble? Yes. Why are we doing this? Years and years will pass before we are enlightened.

But there is one subject that has to be gone into right now: *names*.

Names are more than just a way to identify ourselves. Many ancient people from the kind of world which we (unknowingly) were about to enter had two names—one for everyday and the other for special occasions. Oddly enough, our beautiful, old names—Elizabeth (me) and Eleanor (your grandmother)—were almost never used. I was always Betty and she was Sis, which we both hated.

When our adventure began, we thought briefly of going back to Elizabeth and Eleanor, but somehow it didn't fit, so we waited and waited, calling each other just plain *you* until one day (which you'll hear about later) I became Rusty and she became Sandy. Like people of old, I have always kept Rusty a secret, using it only for the special occasions when we'd take our trips. Your grandmother, on the other hand, has used Sandy all the time from the moment it appeared, keeping Sis the deep, dark secret.

Since, as perhaps you can discern already, we are at once very alike and very different, we decided that the only way to tell our tale was one at a time—first one voice and then the other. Since you've heard mine, it's time now to hear your grandmother's.

SANDY

The 1930s. I arrived in New York. Steam burst from the train and blinded me as I stepped down to the platform. I opened my eyes and there she stood.

She was about my age and tall, with the darkish red hair

that seems to catch minute changes of color and light. I had been told that she was scholarly and expected to be rendered speechless, but Rusty's brilliance is not intimidating. It is star-brilliant and magnetic. It enthralled and tempted me immediately and, after more than sixty years, still does—only much more so. At that very first meeting we *knew* one another; we were at ease, with a strange undercurrent of excitement.

I had met her brother at a wedding in Michigan and found in him everything I wanted and nothing I could resist: marvelous good looks, rare intelligence and sensitivity, astonishing wit and the promise of adventure.

A few months after meeting him, we met in Washington and he proposed to me upon a compost pile at Mount Vernon. I accepted with my whole heart.

So, there I was on that train platform in New York, faced with my sister-in-law-to-be. She would proceed to shake up my life.

PART ONE

Chapter 1

RUSTY

Magic undoubtedly hovered over us from the first moment, but we did not feel it—not yet. For six years we attended to our destinies as wives, housewives and mothers. We continued to encounter one another (we were, after all, sisters-in-law), and we always rejoiced in one another's company. But magic? No.

And then, in the early fall of '41, we went to Canada.

We chose Canada because it was convenient, but why we chose to go on a trip I cannot now recall except that I was low in my mind and confused. As Dante remarked, "The direct way was lost." As if I had ever found it.

Sandy was not lost, but she was down—most of all, adventure-less. She sensed the possibility of some kind of happening with me.

Little did she know. We drove from Detroit across the bridge to Windsor, Ontario. And it all began.

Everything sparkled: the sky, the trees, even the city streets. Granted, the weather was perfect, the leaves were turning and Canadian cities are startlingly clean compared to ours, but it was more than that. It was our first exposure to environmental magic. Now we are so accustomed to this that we see with double vision.

Places exist, streets have names and can be found, restaurants sell food that (usually) can be eaten, hotels have rooms with beds and bureaus sitting on rugs. But a delicate, glittering gauze curtain subtly alters the world. As in the ballet, well-constructed scenery can still be glimpsed when the gauze is lowered. It is there all right, but it is not germane.

Talk. We talked and talked and talked, about ourselves mostly, but I always have trouble putting limits to things. In the beginning Sandy resisted me intellectually, which is not to be wondered at. I am a compulsive radical who (using the word correctly) digs down to roots even if it ploughs up the lawn and undermines nice, safe, surrounding walls. I was a threat to Sandy's security. I never resisted her. There was no need to. I already shared her sense of the presence of Something Other. What she put in the kitty was a fizzling melange of excitement and anticipation. I was always and instantly transformed, head-to-toe, by the fireworks she engendered.

It was on this earliest trip that we heard the song "You and I." We heard it everywhere we went and we have ever since recognized an entity known to us as You-and-I. The words are silly and have nothing to do with the You-and-I entity that experienced (and survived) the coming adventures.

And it was here that we were assaulted by our first You-and-I wolf whistle. This was not your run-of-the-mill catcall from a nearby construction worker. It was ear splitting. Furthermore, it issued forth from a large, red face topped by a hard hat, which popped out of a manhole. Though never again quite so dramatic, the high decibel wolf whistle accompanied us like a recurring operatic theme. When it began to fade, we missed it. Badly.

"But shouldn't we have felt harassed?" Sandy recently wondered.

We should have, of course. After all, as time passed, we both became card carrying, tireless upholders of women's rights. Moreover, our daughters are professionals and, in youth, tended to wear T-shirts with statements such as "Men of quality are not threatened by women for equality." Nonetheless, the wolf whistle was always, for us, a thermometer registering our general effect.

I once asked my very conservative British father what he thought of wolf whistles in general (not of course those directed at his daughter and his daughter-in-law).

"They belittle women," he promptly replied.

So the whole spectrum, right to left, condemns wolf whistles; just not Rusty and Sandy. When the whistle was accompanied by invitations ranging from the decent to the decadent, we didn't even toss our heads disdainfully, much less summon the authorities. The whistlers and the whistlees just found it cheering.

SANDY

Now when I look back on that first trip, I begin to see why it took so long to realize what was happening. Both of us had to change before we could even begin to understand what was in store for us and, at least as far as I was concerned, the changes had to be gradual or my mind would have blown in fragments.

Until that first trip with Rusty I was very content, not because I was placid or stupid but because I liked things the way they were. I'd had a wonderful life, loved my family, traveled a lot and spent happy times with animals and in wild places. I had absorbed conventional ideas and beliefs because those were comfortable and had lots of room in them.

Rusty changed all this with her questioning, doubting and discarding—and then reaching for new ideas in brand new territory. It was upsetting to be so upset—it was wonderful, too—but before we could go waltzing off together where angels fear to tread, Rusty had to get me over some pretty silly hang-ups.

This began on our second trip.

Jamaica was the battleground.

First, the airport. Because it is easier to say yes than no, I often promise to do things that I will not or cannot do, trusting that when the time comes, plans will change or I will be dead. So I told Rusty that I would fly to Jamaica, knowing it would be impossible because I have, or did have, a severe fear of flying.

The morning we were to leave, I was sprightly and enthusiastic until the flight was announced. I then hid in the ladies' room. Rusty panicked, finally found me and dragged me to the gate. By that time, there was such an uproar that I had to go because another of my hangups was fear of making a scene. Thus, Rusty dealt with two problems and realized there were more where those came from.

We arrived in Jamaica, which in the 1940s was still glorious and unspoiled. I felt wonderful, but not for long.

One afternoon Rusty said, "Just for fun, tell me what things embarrass you." Unsuspecting, I said, "Doing cheesy things and wearing cheesy things." Cheesy is what we used to call anything we considered bad taste.

I was dragged off to the nearest tourist shop, the kind that embarrasses me even to think about. There, God help us, Rusty bought me an ankle bracelet with a dangling map of Jamaica and challenged me to wear it.

I had survived the plane trip and the dreadful scene preceding it, and Earth was not altered the night we went on the town with me in an ankle bracelet. I even became quite heady and told Rusty I really had never liked Gilbert and Sullivan or Currier and Ives.

Several innocently happy days passed, but I should have suspected that there was more to come. Rusty had once spent an entire year studying philosophy. Obviously, I was not going to escape the result.

My general approach to off-the-track talk was to take a prissy sip of my martini, if happily one was handy, or at least to try changing the subject. If all else failed, I fell back on my belief in a personal, loving God I really didn't want to talk about.

Then on an afternoon I vividly remember, we sat on the beach and what should appear but the Ten Commandments. Since I had given it little thought (and, like most people, couldn't possibly name all ten), what Rusty had to say was fascinating. In fact, I hung by a thread until the thread snapped and we began to laugh—not giggles or tittles or anything that might be described as polite mirth. We hooted and howled, tried to stop, wheezed into our bath towels and finally succumbed from exhaustion.

Now there is absolutely nothing funny or even mildly entertaining about the Ten Commandments. Nothing. Yet we shook with laughter. Out-of-the-blue recurrences were to fell us quite regularly in time to come. Now we know it isn't so much that we shake as that we are shaken.

Looking back, I seem to see that long-ago afternoon as a sort of map of what was to come: Rusty brimming over with her learning, me struggling to keep fences in place, and both of us swept away in an unnerving, inexplicable, and totally joyous hysteria.

I've always had a lust for adventure. I certainly don't mean scaling mountains or crossing the ocean alone in a sailboat. I mean that many things which happen to me are not quite what one would expect. Just going to the grocery store can involve a strange meeting, a bizarre accident or the beginning of a trail of odd events.

My children always loved doing things—even just shopping—with me, because "something always happens." But when real adventure tempted with wild trimmings, I could never find anyone who would go along.

Then, Rusty appeared in my life—and she will go as far as I. When our gears enmeshed and You-and-I went into overdrive, both of us began to feel invincible and that's well on the way to being invincible.

RUSTY

So what is the adventure?

We are being sought—and this seeking has been going on for years and years, in fact for decades.

Now you may suspect from what you know of us, Melanie, that your grandmother and great-aunt are not your typical easily classified, run-of-the-mill American citizens. On the other hand, we obviously function well enough to get by. Who, in other words, would ever suspect that Something Other had crossed or lifted or broken a barrier to get at us?

We know now what that Something is—only it's not a Something, it's a Someone.

It has been many, many years since those first trips of ours, but we are still regularly staggered by the drama in which, willy-nilly, we continue as participants. How does it work?

Like this: We leave on a trip. Since we live far apart this is not always easy, but at last money is in hand, the scene chosen, the accommodations made, family problems solved. (Our families, though never enthusiastic, gradually became reconciled to what they perceived as baffling but inevitable.)

The first morning, dressed to the teeth, we set forth.

***

Now that we are old...well, we're more than old now. Since for me youth ends at 25, middle age at 50 and old age at 75, I see us in that parlous limbo contributed by modern medicine. Well, all right, now that we are ancient we are no cynosure—yet even today eyes stray to us.

But in our middle years—our adventures began in our late 20s—we were clearly magnetic. Of course we formed a somewhat peculiar pair, a sort of Alpha and Omega: Sandy small, sparky and very pretty, with the blonde hair that gentlemen prefer; I tall, slender, a once-upon-a-time redhead, very cool (the impression given, not the fact) and, I was often told, "almost beautiful." From time to time someone of particular discernment (or perhaps only in a bad light) would obligingly go so far as to leave out the "almost."

Well, let's face it. Both of us were, in the tribal custom of our day, among the "Debutantes of the Year."

We were, as we stepped down the street, in a state of hyper-something. We knew it and so did everyone who happened to see us. Many years were to pass before we discovered what it was.

One of the earliest, oddest, and most persistent trip phenomena was (and is) sneezing. We sneeze almost immediately upon meeting, and soon we begin to hear loud, out-of-control sneezes all around us.

Another equally peculiar and early phenomenon was the appearance of hearses. At times, it was so constant that we wondered if the city where we happened to be had been overtaken by some obscure health problem. When nobody else appeared even mildly distressed, we too assumed the mantle of indifference. After all, hearses are not exactly inspiring. In time, this particular vision seemed to dwindle away, or at least to lose its persistence.

The hearses, however, and the sneezing, though plenty startling, were not candidates for Most Important Aspect of our trips. That was, and remains, the inner conviction that we were secure wherever and whenever we were. Wherever was simply a place we chose to wander—any place at all. Granted, the world was a safer place then than now, but it sure as hell wasn't perfectly safe. You-and-I, however, were never at risk. We were protected (and of course, if you're protected there's a Protector, isn't there?) Whenever was dawn or dusk, night or day. Time never hemmed us in. Wine was part of the joy: the barrier breaking, the egg laying which made up You-and-I. But we never got in any kind of trouble. Protected? Of course we were. Completely.

Imagine setting forth to look for something without having a clue what or where it was! Our times together have always been a treasure hunt—or, as we later saw it, a paper chase. But trails are laid, are they not?

They are indeed, and we grasped that early on. The layer we called the Cosmics in the beginning—plural because it was important to remind ourselves we were not dealing with anything that might even remotely be identified as Almighty or Primal Force.

We always knew that You-and-I was made up of more than the two of us. Paper chases begin with something that catches our eye—often, but not always, in store windows—and then is repeated and repeated. When we are "getting warm" the excitement increases. We talk, searching, prodding, going off the rails (which we quickly grasp), taking a new tack, picking up the tracks in a different place and context. And then, at last, we *know*. Eureka! What has appeared is a symbol for our contemplation, education and delectation.

We repair to the nearest public library to look up the symbol's significance. Oohs and aahs, snorts of barely stifled mirth and gasps of wonder have troubled library silence from

Dan to Beersheba. Librarians have also been disturbed by the quirkiness of our requests and our unfathomable goals. But, by and large, they've been game—even, on occasion, heroic: searching on hands and knees for dusty treasures in the dark corners of bottom shelves. With the passage of time, the mythology, magic and mysticism section of my own library has grown so enormously that I can do further research at home. That we are not in command is made blindingly clear over and over and over again. The symbols are always foreign to us, each significance unknown.

The circle was the first, presented to us in the form of a carousel: the Merry-Go-Round, a bar at Copley Plaza in Boston. We became more or less obsessed with the place, sensing somehow that it was enchanted ground, yet not having a clue as to how or in what way. It seemed something was required of us. We chewed at it, argued, dug and dug and delved and delved. What, if anything, was the meaning of circles? Off we went on our first excursion to the public library, fumbled about and finally came up with the right books—our introduction to symbolism. Wow!

Circle: solar eye, infinity, deity, eternity, completeness, continuity. Emblem of the Zoroastrian god Ormuzd and the Greek/Roman god Hermes/Mercury.

"Anything else? While we're here?"

"Wine, maybe? After all, the Merry-Go-Round is a bar."

Wine: elixir of eternal life, good fellowship, inspiration, mirth, resurrection, salvation, spiritual blessing, wisdom. Sacred to Dionysos/Bacchus.

What now? It was of course a gorgeous day (it always is, even when nobody else would think so). We walked and talked and talked and walked and made up our minds we should buy something to celebrate. Clearly, it had to be round. Something to hang on the wall? No, we decided, something to hang on ourselves—pendants.

Then of course we had to spend time pondering what should be engraved on the pendants. A message seemed important or at least a comment. We pondered this both together and apart and finally settled on *Ne Plus Ultra*, but without the *Ne*—i.e. *This Far and Further*. *Plus Ultra* would go on one side, on the other a unicorn.

The unicorn, though in fact the second of our symbols, was the first we instantly recognized as such. We didn't even have to talk about it. We just knew. After being presented to us, this beautiful creature became nauseatingly familiar, prostituted by merchants and media; but when we first encountered him, he was rare—at least alone.

Facing the lion on the British coat of arms, the unicorn is, of course, renowned. But we saw his outline on an old building, a piece of pottery, then a tapestry. We fell in love.

Much research has revealed the following: He is a moon symbol and therefore a symbol of femininity. On the other hand he represented to the alchemists the virile force of the *spiritus mercurialis*. Recognizing this ambiguity, alchemists decided he had a double nature and dubbed him *Monstrum Hermaphroditum*.

Alchemy is fascinating, but hardly a reason to fall in love. It was his fearlessness, his daring, his swiftness that charmed. I was drawn to his solitude, Sandy to his wisdom. Both of us were drawn to his magic. All over the world and all through history, he has championed kindliness, nobility, the individual—and though he always has one horn, he can alter its shape along with his own. The sun alone, whom the ancients saw as a lion, is his enemy—forever wrestling the unicorn to his knees, but never defeating him decisively. All the animal world, except the lion, acknowledges him as lord—as did much of the human world in older and more poetic times. To the Zoroastrians he stood at the right hand of Ormuzd, creator of all things bright and beautiful.

So back to the pendants.

We looked up silversmiths in the Boston Yellow Pages. (Yes, we were back in that enchanted city.) Through the years we have frequently consulted Yellow Pages here and there, almost always with somewhat striking results. The Pendant Episode was no exception. We chose a name of a silversmith completely at random.

The building was shabby but not derelict, so after perusing the registry (fourth floor back), we entered the small, grubby lobby. A figure stood before us: a pleasant faced, late-middle-aged man in a good, though shabby, Harris tweed coat. But it was neither the face nor the tweed that riveted us to the spot, for grasping the lapels he flung the garment wide and gleefully exposed himself in a state of rising enthusiasm.

Luckily, the elevator appeared and we scurried in. Two couples followed us and the doors slammed. Shortly, we would have preferred the lobby.

The elevator stopped near the second floor, but not at the second floor. The climb was at least three feet. With perfect aplomb, the first couple disembarked, the man hauling his dumpy companion with some difficulty but no apparent distress or even surprise.

Stunned, we observed a repetition on the third floor—no astonishment, no resentment. At the fourth floor we tried to step up with dignity—or even without. When this proved impossible, we crawled up and over on our hands and knees.

Disheveled and discombobulated, we found and entered a large studio containing a tall, bony occupant with masses of writhing hair: a sort of cheerful, shock-headed Peter.

"Oh dear," he said, helping us to beat the dust off our good coats. "The elevator?"

We nodded.

"It's often that way in mid-week," he explained. "What's today?"

"Wednesday."

"Well, there you are."

It was instantly apparent to us that we had come to the right place. We were, in other words, connected. Contact had been achieved. A request for pendants with *Plus Ultra* on one side and unicorns on the other would be all in the day's work. He quickly sketched his ideas. We were entranced.

"Now you'll want chains, won't you?"

"Chains?"

"To anchor him—round and round your wrists. Here, take this."

He handed us a giant spool with what appeared to be miles of gorgeous, glittering silver chain. It was impossible not to pull on it, dangle it, wind it, which we did somewhat maniacally, feeling at this point that "anything goes" was the way to go. Four feet seemed about right—eight altogether. Our host agreed and we left him in a "this can't be happening" mood that was to become increasingly familiar.

SANDY

Here I sit and think about this incredible adventure that has befallen us. Here I sit and think.

Rusty copes with cold. I have softness, warmth, azaleas, dogwood and moss. I heard the first whippoorwill last night. He's early this year.

As I look out of the window I see many animals either wild or rescued. I am very, very lucky to live on this wilderness island where people are fenced in and the land belongs to the animals that can come and go as they please.

I see three dogs: one was abandoned here on the island by hunters, one was to have been killed because a pedigreed bitch had a mixed litter so proper papers were out of the question. The third dog was found on the highway on the mainland, lost and starving.

My 12 geese were left in a small pond when the owners of the land moved away. Thirteen Muscovy ducks were sent to me because a neighbor complained about their hissing. We rescued a baby donkey abandoned by its mother. Five deer come for food. A pig dropped by a hawk was mended and brought up on a bottle.

And so it goes.

I marvel, watching from my window. There are lots of fights indeed: fights over food and territory and even just for fun, but never fights over theology. The wild creatures—deer, hogs, raccoon, mink, alligators, snakes and birds—should be a revelation to people. They are at home in the world. They know how to cope with weather, scarcity of food, aggression and, most important of all, over population. When food is scarce, many females do not breed. Wild animals live in adequate structures, handle what they have to handle to survive. They are not pretentious, guilty or power crazy. They don't even overeat.

Even when I was a child and a copycat Protestant, I hated having to swallow this quote from the Bible: "Be fruitful and multiply, and replenish the earth and subdue it: and have dominion over the fish in the sea, and over the fowl of the air, and over every living thing that moveth upon the earth."

This seems to me an unreasonable statement to be made by an all-knowing deity who certainly must have had an inkling even then how man would turn out.

Animals do not seem to fear death. They fear savagery and the threat of being killed, of course, but, unlike us, they do not appear apprehensive at the prospect of death.

Because of her love for Walt Whitman and animals, Rusty's husband once gave her what remains her favorite Christmas present. It hangs on her wall, decorated with vignettes of those animals most dear to her and, in beautiful calligraphy, these lines from *Song of Myself*:

> I believe a leaf of grass is no less than the journeywork of the stars,
> And the pismire is equally perfect, and a grain of sand, and the egg of a wren,
> And the tree-toad is a chef-d'oeuvre for the highest,
> And the running blackberry would adorn the parlors of heaven,
> And the narrowest hinge in my hand puts to scorn all machinery,
> And the cow crunching with depress'd head surpasses any statue,

> And a mouse is miracle enough to stagger sextillions of infidels
>
> I think I could turn and live with animals, they are so placid and self-contain'd;
> I stand and look at them long and long.
>
> They do not sweat and whine about their condition;
> They do not wake in the dark and weep for their sins;
> They do not make me sick discussing their duty to God;
> Not one is dissatisfied—not one is demented with the mania of owning things;
> Not one kneels to another nor to his kind that lived thousands of years ago;
> Not one is respectable nor unhappy over the whole earth.

When I was young I felt immortal. Death was so far ahead that I rarely gave it a thought. Now when it's just around the corner it's another matter. I do not fear it intellectually but I have not been too pleased by the current encouragement of senility by medical means. Also, I used to be quite chicken, and wondered secretly how I would cope with such a journey. Embarked on Rusty's and my Incredible Adventure, I see that Here and There are never what they seem.

I dearly loved a magnificent woman here on my island, Queenie Mae Williams. I knew her for seventy years. When I was a child, she meant comfort without luxury, security because of confidence, joy because of happiness. As I grew older we had adventures and long talks about things that most people know nothing about.

She was different and real with old, unchanging ways and an old, nondestructive approach to life. I suppose there was a memory in her of her long ago, far away African life. She was vivid, interesting, exciting and everlastingly loving.

Then later (Oh Joy, Oh Rapture!) she shared with me a bawdy heart and a lusty soul. She sang spirituals on this island that would make your heart sing and your knees buckle. She had been a blues singer in Savannah and for years had brewed her own brand of corn likker.

She had a blissful common-law husband with one leg whom she treasured and badgered. Every other weekend, with her blessing, he went to Savannah to "hump the sisters." I adored him.

Queenie gradually and thoughtfully taught me many things. I was proud. She taught me that on Christmas Eve every cow in the field knelt down at midnight. Amazingly enough, I found this clipping this past holiday in the *Farmers Consumers Market Bulletin*:

> I want to thank everyone who responded to my letter inquiring as to whether cows get up, turn around and lay back down at midnight on New Year's Eve. According to the responses I received, cows really do this, and one individual said that cows also kneel on Christmas Eve. One person said they had watched this every year since childhood, but the past four years his cows did nothing on either holiday.
>
> Iona Jones

Queenie taught me things about healing, prevention of illness and trouble. Most exciting of all were our trips to town to a store that sold potions, oils, herbs, roots, and candles. Underlying everything was her faith, as firm as Mount Olympus. Today, I would give a lot to have that faith.

Nevertheless, I still have my potions in a handmade cedar box. Healing oil, protection oil, five fingers grass, life everlasting buds, commanding oil, peaceful home, protecting and commanding oil, lodestone, High John the Conqueror, Lo John the Conqueror, buckeye.

Why not? Who can possibly know what is important and what is not? What's the difference between High John the Conqueror and Christian or Muslim symbols?

As Queenie always assured me, "Whatever blows your frock up" or "Whatever razzes your berry."

RUSTY

Queenie was not the only dearly beloved female whose life affected us both. There was also my Aunt Katharine, known as "Auntie Kay" to the family and "Miss P." to us. She was your great-great aunt, Melanie, and though you never knew her, you have doubtless heard much about her.

She was a creature blessed in some special, indecipherable way. I have come to believe she was a saint but a very special kind—in a class, perhaps, with Saint Francis. Most of those who have been designated saints by their theologies repulse me. They're always bleeding or fainting, eyes rolled up, everything drooping. I'm sure they never took baths or smiled or allowed themselves a night out. I suggested this once to Miss P. who said, "Now, darling, you must not say things like that" before dissolving into giggles.

Simone Weil once defined love as the giving of attention. Miss P. gave her attention—all of it—to anyone who needed her. And it was fascinating to Miss P. watchers to observe how people of either sex and any age never knew how much they needed her until they got to know her and then found they couldn't do without her. My brother and I fought over her. Our sons, when we were all together in summer, joined forces to capture her, luring her into their room and locking out our daughters. The girls, of course, retaliated.

With the patience regularly assigned to saints, she would play complex and (to us) obscure games with the boys. The girls must have been even more of a trial. One whole summer, I remember, they were horses and spoke in neighs, Miss P. obliged to respond in kind. It is probably not necessary to add that animals instantly recognized her and glued themselves to her side.

She could have invented the concept of extrasensory perception, knowing when things were not right no matter how distant the sufferer. "Your aunt," people used to say, "is magical."

Yes she was, but nobody would guess it at first. She could best be described as ladylike—quietly dressed, soft-spoken, every hair in place. Her face was peaceful, her bearing aristocratic—until suddenly she would do her "Italian fight," turning into two furious Neapolitans intent on murder. She was a passionate reader, but kept her knowledge and wisdom largely hidden lest it "put someone down." As far as I know she never made a moral judgment. She didn't need to. Without trying, she drew out the goodness in people. She was no Pollyanna, yet somehow you knew tangles would be straightened out.

The moment she and Sandy met they appeared to be already well acquainted and they remained that way until death did them part.

You-and-I, needless to say, entranced her and we relived our adventures in our private Show-and-Tell time, capturing her as greedily as the children did. Through her eyes we saw lights and shapes in You-and-I that somehow enhanced it.

SANDY

Here is a last glimpse of Miss P.: She had an extraordinary relationship with alcohol. She used to drink Old Fashioned with all the fixings—mixed and poured correctly—but exceedingly potent to our wondering eyes. Never did she so much as sag in her chair or slur a letter. It was awesome. Why—and how—we wondered, did she always remain completely sober?

When World War II was on and our husbands were overseas, she used to say, "If the boys both come home safe and sound, I'm going to get drunk."

They did, and we reminded her of her promise. We all sat around in the living room and drank. While four of us became increasingly disabled, Miss P. sat bolt upright, dark eyes shining, her lovely face aglow with joy, and smiled upon us.

RUSTY

Some kind of contact between You-and-I and our Something Other, totally mysterious, totally unexpected, was—and is—always made, but not always in the same fashion. Sometimes it comes about through visible, tactile symbols, sometimes through compulsions (or propulsions) like the pendant episode, and sometimes through messages. Once upon a time, we used to tip tables frequently and with great success.

With equal success we sought out psychics, visited readers of palms, tea leaves and the Tarot, and questioned the I Ching—but none of this works any more. The barrier between Here and There has been leveled by a hand far more powerful.

Table tipping was taught us by our grandmothers. With hands lightly on a table top the table may tip as letters of the alphabet are called—thus making words.

On one occasion we asked where we should go next on a trip.

"Arcadia," said the table.

We talked and pondered and argued—and finally got out the map. Wildly excited, we discovered that Nova Scotia, easily reached, was Arcadia! And off we went. Yes, of course we soon discovered Nova Scotia was Acadia, but one little bitty 'r' seemed unimportant.

Our entire visit was blanked out by fog.

"Mist? Mist, Mist," mused Sandy, and then she shrieked "MISSED!"

Presto! We knew that contact had been made. Puns were—and are—the particular joy of—hang on, Melanie, you'll find out in due time.

***

Time marched on. Sometimes we skipped a year, sometimes we were able to meet more than once in a twelvemonth, but whether the trips lasted ten days (rare), five (the usual), or, on one occasion, a few hours, something always happened.

SANDY

That few hours trip is worth describing. It was not a trip in our usual use of the word. Rusty and I just happened to be in New York on the same day and we decided to meet, even though we had exactly two hours away from other plans and responsibilities.

We met on Fifth Avenue in front of one of those sad, thirsty trees planted in the sidewalk. We had nothing specific in mind—we never do—but we felt a high wave of excitement—we always do.

Soon, a shop down the side street came in focus. It had a window of East Indian jewelry, bright fabrics and small figurines. It was nothing extraordinary and neither of us is particularly fond of such shops. However, in we went.

Shelves and tables and counters were jammed with small animal figures of many kinds. There wasn't much time. What were we being shown? I bought a small, weird bird inlaid with turquoise and coral. We felt we had to buy something because we had just been standing around, staring into space, and the proprietor was less and less pleased. Rusty bought a cloth bull spangled with mirrors, embroidery and orange tassels.

"So what?" you might ask.

But wait! These weren't realistic animals. All the creatures jammed on all the shelves looked mythical. Maybe...the ark?

We rushed in our remaining half hour to a bookstore and pounced upon a Bible to read about the flood. Nothing jumped out to explain the wild excitement we knew so well. We had to part.

But when Rusty got home and looked up the ark, there was the message. It seems that both materially and spiritually, the ark is a symbol of preservation and rebirth. There are strange and intriguing beliefs that essences of both the physical and the spiritual can be compressed in a time of crisis and held safely within a small space until time for rebirth.

The symbolist René Guernon sees a connection between Noah's ark and the rainbow that signaled all was well. Both figures together, he surmised, complete a circle of Oneness.

We started thinking about rainbows. We have seen rainbows on almost every trip—strange, long-lasting, brilliant, unexpected. We have seen double rainbows—once, unbelievably, a rainbow like a ring, directly overhead.

So what is a rainbow?

It is, old sources say, a bridge connecting the perceived with the unperceived. And in parts of long ago Africa, the rainbow expressed the desire of the gods to approach—or at least communicate with—the denizens of earth. Could anyone possibly come up with a better You-and-I symbol?

RUSTY

Next in impact and importance to unicorns and carousels and rainbows—and perhaps the greatest of our paper chases—came "The Owl and the Pussy Cat."

This revelation took place throughout one long, sparkling day when time, as it often does, stood still and we were alone in a magic city—known to the man on the street as Boston. Small guitars leapt at us along with nose rings and seascapes and mysterious trees and banks and money and jars of honey.

Suddenly, with a joyful shout and momentarily clutching each other for security, because it's scary as well as marvelous, we saw it. After a brief search for a runcible spoon—a beautiful, entirely useless object—we discovered, just at closing time, a volume of Edward Lear's poetry, plus a long biography. Very strange and magic, we learned, were both he and his Owl and Pussy Cat. The alchemist's vision of the unicorn had been our first encounter with the far-out and infinitely significant world of androgyny. The Lear poem was our second. No personal pronouns, you see, are applied to the Owl or the Pussy Cat. And, searching for further information, we learned that, symbolically speaking, both creatures are the messengers of witches.

I know you learned the poem in infancy, Melanie, but here it is anyway:

I

The Owl and the Pussy Cat went to sea
  In a beautiful pea-green boat,
They took some honey and plenty of money
  Wrapped up in a five-pound note.
The Owl looked up to the stars above

And sang to a small guitar,
O lovely Pussy, O Pussy, my love,
What a beautiful Pussy you are,
You are
You are!
What a beautiful Pussy you are!"

II
Pussy said to the Owl, "You elegant fowl,
How charmingly sweet you sing!
Oh! let us be married: too long have we tarried:
But what shall we do for a ring?"
They sailed away, for a year and a day,
To the land where the bong-tree grows;
And there in the wood a piggy-wig stood,
With a ring at the end of his nose,
His nose,
His nose,
With a ring at the end of his nose.

III
"Dear Pig, are you willing to sell for a shilling
Your ring?" Said the Piggy, "I will."
So they took it away, and were married next day
By the turkey who lives on the hill.
They dined on mince and slices of quince,
Which they ate with a runcible spoon;
And hand in hand, on the edge of the sand,
They danced by the light of the moon,
The moon,
The moon,
They danced by the light of the moon.

"The hermaphrodite," wrote Robertson Davies, "though a freak in nature, is psychologically a representation of completeness, of unity."

Serpents, for example, entered our lives on Captiva Island—famous for shells and not snakes, for Pete's sake. There were gorgeous entwined serpents on a bottle of new de Saint Phalle perfume, serpents painted on fans, carved on driftwood canes, on pottery—everywhere. Nobody noticed. Nobody ever does. So here is the dope on serpents:

They are, first and foremost, symbolic of androgyny, their various meanings all in contradictory pairs: death and regeneration, destruction and guardianship, circles and lightning, divinity and worldliness, pleasure and grief, wisdom and jealousy, brazen power and subtlety.

Another androgynous symbol that has pursued us—or rather, sprung up before our eyes—again and again and in a variety of places is the bell. It only takes a quick look to see bells are a sexually androgynous symbol, but they are much more than that. They ring for birth and death, for morning and night, for grief and joy, for disaster and victory.

Along with bells, purple presents itself to us persistently. In the world of color, purple is unmistakably androgynous, standing as it does for glory and mourning, splendor and tragedy, arrogance and wisdom. In white magic, it is used for altruistic purposes; in black magic, for destructive ends.

SANDY

Sometimes our trips were hardly earth-shaking, Melanie. But however cheery, or just plain frivolous, we were always,

always, always a trio—in other words, two of us simply went where we were directed by the third. And again, there was always, always, a message. It might range from the exalted or even earth shaking to the purely giggly, but it was there, unexpected yet recognizable.

On a visit to the Florida Naples, we were proffered a mole. For some reason we can't now recall, we knew right away that further mole research should be pursued in a bookshop: specifically, in the children's section of a bookshop.

The proprietor was exceedingly stout; he was also, he informed us, arthritic.

"Could you tell us where to find *Appley Dappley's Nursery Rhymes*?" Rusty asked. "We need to look up 'Diggory Delvet.' "

Well, I knew she was on the wrong track because I was absolutely positive what we wanted was "One, two, buckle my shoe."

"Mother Goose is what we really need," I said firmly. The proprietor looked at us over the top of his glasses—two all-dressed-up ladies not in their first youth, arguing about moles.

"All the poetry books are underneath the children's section," he told us. "But I can't get under there myself."

We looked dubiously at a space about two feet high, but when we are called we go. No choice. We tried reaching under the shelf on our hands and knees, but in the end had to do it on our stomachs. The dust was thick, the heat horrendous, but we got the books.

> Diggory, Diggory Delvet,
> A little old man in black velvet;
> He digs and he delves –

You can see for yourselves
The mounds dug by Diggory Delvet.

"That's it," Rusty said. Triumphantly, I held up Mother Goose. "One, two, buckle my shoe," and at last, "eleven, twelve, dig and delve!"

"Digging and delving is certainly what moles do and it's certainly what we've been doing, are doing and are obviously supposed to go on doing," announced Rusty, "so either rhyme will do."

But she soon had to face the fact that Mother Goose won the blue. Our hotel room number was eleven twelve.

Chapter 2

RUSTY

After the very light of You-and-I went up, we began to see ourselves as alike. So did outsiders. We were taken for relatives, sisters, and—finally and most fantastically—as twins. The stranger who saw us in this guise walked over to our restaurant table as we consumed dessert (we knew he had been staring since salad) and looked closely at us: me with lightly freckled skin and reddish hair, she with lightly tannish skin and yellow hair.

"Rusty and Sandy: the Desert Twins. Sounds like a book," he intoned, and wove off.

But we are not alike, though we share some basic elements which made it easy for the Powers That Be—known to us originally as the Cosmics—to get the show on the road.

We are upper income WASPs, both native to the U.S. of A. and more or less of an age. Presumably, had They so desired, the Cs could have woven our lives together had one of us been a Hottentot and one an Eskimo.

In that case, were we singled out simply because we were handy when They decided to begin their experiment? Adventure? Revelation? And when was the beginning? When my brother met Sandy at a party in Michigan? When we were born? When the Cosmics were born?

Hastily, I retrace my steps. Some questions are clearly unanswerable, but though we don't know all—or maybe even half— there are still wondrous tales to tell.

But first it does seem that the pair of human participants should be portrayed, however sketchily.

Sandy is not sure. She asks, "Why not let us emerge piecemeal as the story unfolds?"

But I don't see it that way. We already were when we were picked out. Chosen people are chosen people. They are this particular shape and size. Also, it's tricky and tiring to fit revealing tidbits into a text so they don't stick out.

"Well, all right," she says.

Do I want to do this? Do I want to do any of this? Not much, nor does Sandy, which is of no consequence. Sitting here more than 60-odd years after our first meeting I am compelled, and she's trapped along with me.

I said to Sandy, "What is the purpose of this book?"

"Since nothing that has happened to us was our choice, how do we know?" she replied.

And then she added, "There's one thing I do know for sure and that's that there had to be two of us. At times things have been so overwhelming that one would have perished."

Beyond our native WASP-ishness and a more or less similar envelope of Time and Space, we share one trait basic to everything that has befallen us. Because we are perpetually, goose-fleshingly alert to the possible presence of Something Other, we are both astounded by life and can always be stopped in our tracks as we trudge the daily round.

Yet within these samenesses we are not the same. Both of us are reasonably intelligent, but Sandy's intelligence could perhaps better be called wisdom while mine is a firecrackery kind of intellectualism that ignites at the drop of a new idea and blasts off in all directions.

I seem to be without the proper quota of instincts, and rarely know how to live from day to day. I am a sojourner, endlessly ruminating, cogitating, and speculating to discern what role to play. This has an up as well as a down side. I'm good on a stage—acting, lecturing or whatever—making contact with people at a distance. Sandy shudders at the mere thought of a stage. She is at home in the real world—even geographically at home. On our trips I never know where I am and stumble along in her determined wake.

I think it would be safe to say, Melanie, that she sees life through the specific and I through the general. She does not wish to roar through subjects like a fast train through country stations. One might, (all right, I might) say that she wants to know a lot about a little, I a little about a lot.

I gulp while she savors. Both of us write but from polar points of view—she deals with incident, I with the whole canvas. She reacts to the dance step, the branch, the person, the line, the *mot juste*; I to the dance, the forest, humanity, the entire gallery, the whole jammed, crammed library.

Well, actually I don't even stop there. Give me a moment

and I'll drag you through biology, aesthetics, linguistics and (primitive) physics—ultimately abandoning you agasp in the rarefied air of metaphysics while I probably go off somewhere by myself. I have to be alone a lot. In my lexicon, *alone* has never been a synonym for lonely.

Sandy is witty.

"If," said Bernard Shaw, "you find something inexplicable, kindly do not attempt to explain it to me." Sandy's wit is inexplicable. She just turns some kind of shimmering beam upon people and events and—lo! The terrain changes so unexpectedly, onlookers dissolve. Never mind if that's no explanation. It's all I can manage. Sandy's wit springs, I think, from a deep well of light. At the center of Sandy it is always dawn. At the center of Rusty it is twilight.

But twilight isn't darkness. It's just a very different kind of light from dawn. The beam I turn upon people and events is more like an X-ray which leads me through the sensual to the ethereal. I often clearly perceive both objects and happenings that appear barely visible to my fellows.

We both married for love, by which I mean nobody pushed our eventual husbands at us or us at them. I chose a wise and loving man who managed to cope with me for nearly seventy years. Sandy chose my brother—seductive, adventurous, witty, and elusive. Trails of the smitten stretched in a long line behind these two—trails formed practically from the cradle. They returned affection, often lavishly, and Sandy even suffered over the fate of the smitten (my dashing brother rarely, if ever). Married, they instantly became a cynosure. They were real show stoppers—until they broke up.

Animals: she surrounds herself with them—tame, wild

and half-wild. She is a female Francis of Assisi. I too have always lived with furry and feathered friends, but individuals are not my focus. I die over their collective fate, their helplessness in our hands, the awesome stupidity of homo sapiens vis-a-vis his fellow mortals. Sandy cannot bring herself to read of the horrors we perpetrate upon our nonhuman fellows, while I force myself to ponder every last agony, feeling that what they endure I can at least absorb secondhand, keeping the raw side out so I won't belittle and won't forget. Sandy yearns for wilderness and wants always to be in or near it. I too am moved by its beauty and mystery and for that very reason feel that I should probably stay the hell out of it.

Compromise: Sandy can. She can even do it serenely. Obviously life cannot be lived on any other terms, which is why her ship sails the high seas while mine loses its mast, springs leaks, crashes on rocks or rots in doldrums.

I believe, for instance, that at this point nothing and I mean nothing is the slightest use except human population control. Everything else is fiddling while Rome burns. I have also believed, ever since I was a child, that there is never, and again I mean never, any justification for hunting, fishing or the use of laboratory animals.

People sometimes ask me when or how or where these passionate convictions overcame me. I cannot answer. I can't remember ever feeling any other way. Hunting and fishing, which are called sports, appall me as much as laboratories. For me the right definition of sport would be a physical activity entered into either alone or with consenting adversary. Killing for pleasure is not a sport. It's murder. (Those are two "for instances." There are plenty more.)

But is any of this kind of thinking helpful in society? No, it is not, but it doesn't matter so much any more.

"Old age," wrote an old-ager, "is not for sissies, but one of the nice things about it is that you can be eccentric without being considered queer." She is right. Witness this present effort.

Truth: Now, don't resign, Melanie. You've got to stick around because you or anyone else who reads this just has to know who was sought for so many years and so persistently. Says a dictionary on the subject of truth: 1) Conformity with the facts; 2) Ideal or fundamental reality apart from and transcending perceived experience.

Now, as so often results from dictionary excursions, I am enlightened. The first definition is how yours truly would define what did happen on Friday. I don't always tell all, or if I do, I present it suitably dressed. But I always know what occurred. Sandy, however, is an out-and-out number two-er: In order to function well in this field, which she most certainly does, one has to deal with paradox. Choosing some reality that transcends perceived experience is surely the trick of the week, but she pulls it off.

Through the years I have been puzzled, fascinated, astounded and, now that I'm old and crotchety, frustrated. The terrain on the far side of five senses and four dimensions is my terrain, rarely as I (or anyone else) can get there. But making things come out all right—or look all right—by elimination, reconstruction or repositioning bothers me. Where does all the debris go?

Recently, I came upon these words: "To perceive justly leads only to sorrow." I accept this and sweat it out. When things—events, ideas, observations, experiences—are too terrible, when the jungle is too thick or the swamp too dark, I cross as best I can, but the horror is right there, the bottom line, the undercoating. Sandy, on the other hand, somehow turns jungles and swamps into a wonderland where those whose lives touch hers are privileged to dwell. I feel compelled to face the past—both the distant and the just-the-other-day past. Sandy yearns for the remembered past, not for the real past.

That things can be—and frequently are—not what they seem is something we both understand, something basic to the whole of You-and-I. But for me this is to accept the possibility of other interpretations, other lighting effects, not to reject what happened on Friday. Come to think of it, this is a startling reversal of our roles. By and large, Sandy is a far more practical person than I, but when it comes to *history* our roles are abruptly reversed. Well, nobody said You-and-I was an everyday situation.

The thing of it is, you see, that Sandy is an enchantress and what enchantresses do is transform. Good enchantresses bring about good transformations and she is a very, very good enchantress. Five-footers return from her presence ten feet tall. The blind see, the deaf hear and the crippled stride off into the sunset, grinning like Jack-o-lanterns. There is no one remotely like her.

What else?

Food. I was raised on good food and I have always served it, but thinking about it, buying it, cooking it and washing up tends to cloud my existence. Reading a cookbook, my mind departs and the words might as well be in ancient Persian. My general feeling about all this is Shakespearean—"Oh, that this too, too solid flesh would melt." As Americans get more and more involved in—and more and more competitive about—food, they get fatter and fatter. A trip to the A & P is ghoulish.

Recently, I have observed that in bookstores, where I spend much of my life (to the detriment of the family budget), there is now a wall of cookbooks and a wall, at right angles, entirely filled with diet books. Illogically, I love to do special kinds of parties, decorating the house along with the table and usually managing to create at least a little magic (and sometimes a lot).

And Sandy? Well, of course, she loves food, loves to cook, feeds armies cheerfully and isn't turned off by obesity.

That's it then, Melanie: the portraits of your grandmother and your great-aunt as best I can draw them in a limited space. The differences between us must be of enormous importance. You wouldn't think at this late date that any more Roman candles would go up for me, who has been relentlessly chewing away at the mystery of You-and-I ever since it was born, but it now seems that together we are a full keyboard for ? to play on.

SANDY

Well, Melanie, we're getting there. The name (and fame) of the Someone Other is just around the nearest corner now, but a strange trip took place just before the revelation, so here it is:

One November in the 1980s, we set off in high spirits for a trip to New Orleans, a trip planned and anticipated with all the usual excitement.

Recently there was a page-long article in the *New York Times* about the restoration of one of the largest and most beautiful of the plantations on the Mississippi delta. It is now an inn set in surroundings of "rare historic interest with exceptional accommodations." We set off in high spirits. Rusty came to Savannah to spend the night in a hotel so we could fly together to New Orleans.

After dinner that night, we went to our room and found the key was not in Rusty's pocketbook where she had put it. Housekeeping had to come to let us in. The key did not reappear, nor did the stopper in the bath tub function. Housekeeping came again. In the morning the desk clerk forgot our wake-up call and we all but missed the bus to the airport.

We had learned that prankish trip problems usually straighten themselves out. So far, it was fun.

In New Orleans, we rented a car at the airport and set off for the wonderful plantation country, crossing flatland and bayous with gigantic, destructive oil tanks. The rental car left a great deal to be desired. It was old and seemed unreliable, but everything is always all right in the end, we assured one another. We drove and drove. The land became more and more isolated. There were miles and miles between houses—not a car, not a soul.

We reached our destination in the late afternoon. We were very tired. It had been a long day, lots of traveling and nothing to eat. We had missed breakfast at the hotel because of the rushed departure, and after New Orleans we had passed no place at all to buy something for luncheon.

The place was majestic—the magnificent old plantation mansion that one would have created in imagination. However, the huge columns facing the Mississippi were flaking.

Scaffolding and sand blasting equipment were scattered about. The parking space was filled with workmen's trucks. After a search for the office we were told that we were to be in a back annex as the mansion was not yet ready to be occupied.

We were shown to a small, bare room: very small, very uninviting, at the top of rickety stairs. We found one towel but no hangers. It wasn't fun any longer, and we were stunned by the information that the nearest restaurant was 25 miles away.

The kind man who had taken us up to the room saw our desperation and said he would see if he could warm up some leftover lunches. He also said, bless him, that he would bring us a bottle of champagne "to celebrate the evening."

At five-thirty, when I was in the bathtub wondering how we would manage with one towel, he brought two warmed-over casseroles of indeterminate ancestry and a bottle of champagne whose plastic cork knocked a hole in the ceiling when pulled.

The next morning, we toured the plantation house with a charming lady whose ancestors had worked there as slaves.

Things started looking up until we were taken to the basement, where we were reluctantly introduced to a muttering old woman in a ski jacket selling postcards. In spite of her severe dental problems we managed to grasp the utterly depressing statement that her ancestors had owned Holloway.

We cancelled our week's reservation and hurriedly packed everything except my nightgown, which had been taken from the one hanger. Our spirit of adventure was waning.

All of this was almost hateful; nothing like this had

ever happened to us before. Baton Rouge was not far and neither of us had ever been there. We tried to leave, but the car wouldn't start. The kindly man who had brought us the champagne did something knowledgeable to the motor, but suggested that we find a garage in Baton Rouge, which we did upon arrival. We also found out that no one we encountered had any idea why the city was named after a red stick.

When we left Baton Rouge, the scenery was serene. Our spirits struggled to rise. We spent a long time searching for and finding and exploring the river plantations. The most famous one we had saved for the last, and I insisted on seeing it even though we still had to drive back to New Orleans for the rest of the trip. Somehow I knew it was important to visit it, for then everything would be all right.

Finally, there it was, stately and beautiful, at the end of a long oak drive. We stopped at the high, locked gate and read the sign: SOUND HORN FOR ADMITTANCE. The car horn refused to make a sound. It was just too much. It was almost frightening. We didn't feel abandoned, we felt that all this was somehow purposeful.

The worst was yet to come.

Heading back toward the city, clearly came the realization that we had no reservations anywhere and must find some place to stay in New Orleans. After driving for miles we saw a pay phone, where I started calling hotels listed in our guidebook. All were full. Then I tried American Express. Yes, they would find something—call back in a half hour. We drove on, stopped again. Nothing so far, call back in a half-hour. The news was grim, but finally American Express found a motel on North Rampart Street.

In late, late afternoon when we found the place, it was

ghastly. Going through a bare, shabby hall with a registration desk, we were led up sagging stairs to a balcony surrounding a filthy swimming pool. In it were about six inches of scummy water clogged with gum wrappers, cans and paper towels.

Our room was furnished with iron cots and plastic waste baskets. There was no key to the door. A telephone was on a table between the beds with the usual information on how to reach the front desk, room service and outside lines but there was no cord, just the instrument. No key and no communication and absolutely nothing that we could do about it.

Maybe a glass of wine would cheer us. Down we went, sitting on stools in front of a dim bar. We asked for two glasses of dry white wine. Glasses were put in front of us and the bartender reached down, brought up a black hose and squirted yellow liquid into our glasses.

A cab took us out for a queasy seafood dinner, and when we returned a man dripping blood stood in front of our room. He was an architecture student who had been mugged. We could offer nothing but sympathy, so finally he went off to seek the management. We closed our door, jamming it shut with a chair and my hair brush.

Back in Savannah, the last night before parting, we had a wrenching talk until two in the morning. Neither of us can now remember what it was about, but it left us even more drained.

The next day Rusty departed in pouring rain, and when I went to pick up my car in the hotel garage it had a dead battery.

For several months we waited at rock bottom, wistful and wondering. And then, the next spring, we went to Bermuda.

PART TWO

Chapter 1

SANDY

Now we come to it. Contact of some kind had always been made, through all the years. Always. Contact with whom?

Whatever place we choose for a trip becomes magic while we are there. We've been—sometimes several times—to Savannah, Sanibel, Richmond, Jamaica, St. Augustine, San Francisco, Montréal, Nova Scotia, Natchez, New York, Boston, Bermuda, Charleston, Key West, Naples, New Orleans, Washington, D.C. Palm Beach, and Santa Fe.

But the Great Revelation was vouchsafed in Bermuda.

We were, as always, enchanted to be there. We love the sea, the rocks and sand, the narrow, winding roads lined with blazing flowers and the neat plots of vegetables grown everywhere to save the expense of importing. We walked and swam and explored.

For some reason I gradually became obsessed with the idea of going out in a glass bottomed boat. I longed to be able to see deep down into the sea.

Rusty was not in the least interested. "The boat," she said, "will be hot and crowded." However, I was possessed, she gave in and we went. It truly was dreadful. The boat was rickety, jammed with people and smelled of candy bars and diesel fuel. It rang with shrieks and canned music. There was even a drunken man with a camera who insisted on posing embarrassed tourists and taking their picture.

After almost an hour, we reached the reefs. The sea was restless, swirling sand and foam obscured our sight through the glass of the lovely corals and fabulous fish that were beneath us.

We eventually found two seats on a bench and gloomily tried to see through the foggy glass while an interminable loud speaker droned on and on about the coral reef we were supposed to be looking at.

Suddenly, we snapped to attention, hardly crediting our ears.

"Coral," announced the announcer, "is androgynous."

We should, I suppose, be used by now to this kind of shock, but we never are. As usual, nobody else appeared startled—as if a word like androgynous belted out of a speaker on a junky old boat was an everyday occurrence.

Of course, back on dry land, we made straight for the library. Coral, we learned, reproduces both by budding and sexuality. In the latter case, "sperm and eggs come from the same source." The article at this point got a little carried away and informed us out of the blue that earthworms copulate with and fertilize each other.

RUSTY

A day or two later, we trundled by bus to St. George's, strolled about, boarded a yesteryear ship, looked into an old church and then wandered through a museum of horse-drawn vehicles, coaches, barouches, victorias, surreys, governess carts, and a calèche that we particularly admired.

We had lunch and then got to work. We knew that clues had been dropped. We knew something was hovering. We reviewed.

"What about the unicorn, the Owl and the Pussy Cat, and now coral?" I asked. "There's got to be something there. Androgynes? Hermaphrodites?"

And that was it. It hit like a blow. We can still remember the percussion.

"HERMES!" I yelped. "HERMES! HERMES!"

We knew, instantly and inarguably.

We staggered from lunch and the very first shop we came to had a window full of Hermes perfume—particularly, of course, Calèche.

There was too much to talk about, to look up in the library, to ponder and explore. We were thrilled, agape, exhausted, shivery.

We had always known we were not a duet. We also knew that the title Cosmics was a stop-gap, our recognition of a Presence that might or might not become knowable.

Well, now we know.

All right, Melanie, go ahead and ask if we truly believe all this; ask if we believe, for example, as we believe the world is round, that the Greek god Hermes not only revealed himself to us on the island of Bermuda but had been attempting to do so for decades and in a dozen places.

Yes, we do. We have even arrived at a point where his presence in our lives is not as stunning as the length and intensity of his pursuit and the extent of our blindness and deafness.

But maybe blindness and deafness are not the right words. After all, how many people have been pursued by a god? All the pursuing I ever heard of or observed was done by people. Who could possibly be prepared for this kind of thing? On the other hand, who could have been prepared for You-and-I or any of the connected wonders?

One of the first episodes in our unending, post-revelation talks that we clearly recalled was the "MIST, MIST, MISSED!" in Nova Scotia, for obviously the message was not Acadia but Arcadia, never-never land of ancient Greece where Hermes and his son Pan were born.

But there were countless other efforts to reach us. Looking back, we discern a mercurial spirit everywhere.

And after all, why shouldn't Sandy and I meet a god? Many Christians insist both on the nearness and accessibility of their deity. So do Buddhists and all the other hosts of seekers. The great difference here is that in the case of You-and-I, the god did the seeking.

SANDY

Should we tell what it's like to encounter a god? I don't

suppose we can, really, but here's a try.

You go along doing what you're supposed to do, more or less knowing who you are, and assuming that your life, though not necessarily smooth, will probably follow the patterns that have already been established. You may or may not ponder the deity you were told about as a child, but the chances of an actual encounter are so small that you rarely, if ever, give it a thought.

And here's another thing: Whenever you read about people undergoing a mystical experience, it's always a) very, very solemn and b) dressed up recognizably, i.e. Christians encounter Christian figures (or spirits or saints or whatever), Buddhists encounter Buddhist emanations and so on. We, however, were the quarry of a joyful, gorgeous yet pixilated, sky-sized yet comradely, personality about whom we knew absolutely nothing except that he was a god familiar to the ancient Greeks.

The arrival of Hermes in our lives was not just unexpected. It was—and is—indefinable, except in its effect. We are shaken to our soles—and souls—when we know he has appeared. We are overcome, overwhelmed, overpowered. We are also overhauled. Everything is new. Anything can happen, and does.

And what does Hermes get out of it? Maybe just the joy of our joy, the wonder and thrill of our wonder and thrill, maybe just to be recognized, to be known however slightly, or maybe to be appreciated, not slightly but passionately, wholeheartedly, with every fibre of our now-aged beings.

RUSTY

Knowing almost nothing about Hermes, we got to work separately and together. Here, Melanie, is some of the early stuff we gleaned:

He is a wind deity, old sources tell us, but I think it would be more accurate to say *the* wind deity. Speeding through space, hearing the songs of moving air, he discovered (and subsequently revealed) the art of music. He bears nothing so obvious as wings on his back. No, they are on his heels and his hat—but always strong enough to keep him afloat.

Because, riding the winds, he is almost constantly in motion, to the Greeks the sudden stillness that sometimes overtakes a gathering meant "Hermes has alighted" or "Hermes has come in." Even with a foot touching the earth, (I cannot quite imagine him with both feet on the ground), he continues to hear music, carrying his head slightly inclined as if listening to some celestial strain.

And music leads us back to his first adventure, the tiptoeing from his cradle to steal and hide his brother Apollo's cattle. On the return trip, he met an ancient turtle waddling silent across the grass. "Now you will die," Hermes said to the turtle, "but you will sing and be remembered forever."

So saying, he scooped the marrow from the shell, strung reeds end to end, and music rang out at the touch of his fingers. He had created the lyre.

Once more curled in his cradle, Hermes gazed innocently at his furious, accusing brother, Apollo. How, he lisped charmingly, could he—a newborn infant—know anything at all about cattle, much less his brother's cattle?

In the *Homeric Hymns*, that marvelous collection of far-away tales, is a chapter called "To Hermes," which captivated us. It goes something like this: "Apollo laughed ominously, saying, 'Out of your cradle, you fiend of dark night,' and grabbed the baby. Borne aloft in Apollo's arms, Hermes first farted, then wildly sneezed—whereupon Apollo dropped him on the ground."

Was this the source of the sneezing that has so mysteriously and consistently beset us? Of course.

Since even violence did not appease Apollo's wrath, Hermes offered him the lyre. This did the trick, and the brothers became and remained friends.

It was at this moment that the famous caduceus was born. Sealing the friendship, Apollo gave his infant brother a winged staff of gold with power to join those split apart. As a test, Hermes thrust his gift between two raging serpents, who instantly wound themselves around it in peaceful harmony.

"This is the rod of Hermes," reads a translation of Epictetus. "Whatever you touch with it will become gold. Bring sickness or death, poverty, reproach or trial for life—all these things shall be turned to profit."

I find the time element particularly arresting. There is no age problem. A newborn, an adult and an ancient (the turtle) enter the story with their age having no consequence and with neither birth nor death appearing as hurdles, much less barriers.

Apollo, while still under his young brother's spell, taught him not only the ways of the animal world, but the secrets of prophecy, at which point caution appears to have entered in. Although Hermes could henceforth foretell, he was forbidden by his august brother to speak of what he knew.

SANDY

But you can't get a hold on Hermes, though he has certainly gotten a hold on us. For instance, when you think you see his laughing outline, you find that he invented the alphabet. Then, trying to grasp him as a scholar, you discover he's the Chief Messenger of the gods. Just as impressive and even more solemn is his role as Divine Psychopomp. Psycho is the Greek word for soul. Pomp, we discovered, has an obsolete meaning: stately procession. Hermes, in stately procession, leads our souls. Where? To the underworld and also, upon occasion and at his discretion, back to the world whence they came. But he doesn't lead them blindfolded. He possesses, say the old records, knowledge of what is beyond death.

Hearses! Of course! Way back in the beginning, he must have been making an early effort to get our attention. When we remained serenely deaf, he closed off that particular pathway.

But there's no "aha, now we know" about any of this. Just when we begin to think of him as esoteric, he emerges as the god of travelers and the marketplace. As compulsive—or compelled—travelers, we have clearly been doing his thing right from the start. Marketplace? When together, we are lured into stores, or at least store windows, from the moment we set forth.

It dawned on us that the word for Hermes is ambiguous. He ties up to down, in to out, life to death, heaven to earth and probably good to evil, or at least safety to danger, and sanity to madness.

Is Hermes the prototype of androgyny?

RUSTY

Re: androgyny, the time has come. This must be looked into—so make yourself reasonably comfortable, Melanie, and here we go.

Did you know that the androgyne is a very common concept of beginnings—i.e., things used to be whole and, presumably, when time and space came along, broke apart? No, you didn't and neither did I, or your grandmother.

I'm sitting here looking across my great valley—well, actually it's snowing and I can't see much, but, as perhaps you recall, on a clear day you can see hills 60 miles away, as the crow flies.

I am undergoing a sort of nervous pressure about all this and feel that I must beware lest anything slide by me. Brewer's *Dictionary of Phrase and Fable* says that the crow always flies straight to its destination—not very exciting, but, as is my wont, I dutifully followed directions, which ordered me to "see raven." The raven, it seems, pure white at the time and obviously lacking in common sense, told Apollo that his current love, a nymph, was two-timing him whereupon, in a fit of pique, Apollo turned the informant coal black.

Where was I? Yes, androgyny.

In front of me is J. E. Cirlot's strange and marvelous *Dictionary of Symbols* (Philosophical Library, 1962). He alternates the words *hermaphroditism* and *androgyny*, so clearly we're dealing with the same phenomenon.

"Psychologically," he writes, "it must not be overlooked that the concept of hermaphroditism represents a formula (which, like most mythic formulas, is only an approximation) of totality—of the integration of opposites. In other words, it expresses in sexual—and hence very obvious—terms the essential idea that all pairs of opposites are integrated into Oneness."

Monsieur Cirlot feels strongly that we must grasp androgyny as an "intellectual activity which is not in itself connected with the problem of the sexes." The page-long definition ends with the statement, "In Alchemy, the Hermaphrodite plays an important role as Mercury; he is depicted as a two-headed figure, often accompanied by the word Rebis (double thing)." He also remarks *en passant* that Hermes/Mercury's duality gives him free will!

We are clearly in deep waters, but there's no turning back at this point. Are we going to have enough time for this project? *Why did our Enlightenment take so long? Why am I wasting what time is left?* Because this is very, very difficult, and I am ancient.

In front of me are several volumes of Joseph Campbell's *Masks of God: Occidental Mythology* (Penguin, 1964) . If he were alive, I wonder if we could have found in him a listening ear? Probably not. I've never gotten the impression that he had actually experienced Something Other, in the way, for instance, that Arianna Stassinopoulos clearly has in her *Gods of Greece.*

Back to Campbell.

He says, and I've simplified things a bit, that a fundamental idea of all religious disciplines of the first millenium B.C. was that "the inward turning of the mind" would result in a realization that the individual and the universe are one and so also are "the principles of eternity and time, sun and moon, male and female, Hermes and Aphrodite (Hermaphroditus)."

Pretty stunning—but there is an oddity in Campbell's presentation which I'm not at all reluctant to point out. After all, he's juggling thousands of concepts, tales, philosophies etc. from round the world and we've been put down specifically in Greece.

Moreover, we have a direct line.

My point is that Hermes had a lot of trouble getting Aphrodite to bed. She had other fish to fry at the time and he had to hide one of her magic sandals to get her undivided attention. It was their son to whom the great, immortal adventure befell. They called him Hermaphroditus because he was so gorgeous that she wasn't about to let him go out in the world bearing only his father's name (sound familiar? You can't tell me the Greeks are on the historical dust heap).

Anyway, what happened was this: A nymph fell for him heart and soul, so profoundly that she wanted not just to go off in the bushes with him but to be him. Her wish was granted, and Hermaphroditus came to represent oneness. At first it was oneness of male and female, but gradually he came to represent all apparent opposites, from sun and moon to eternity and time.

Incidentally, Cirlot speaks of the moon as "intuition, imagination, magic" and the sun as "reason, reflection, objectivity." He also claims that sun and moon have repeatedly changed sex through the ages. This I like. It's warming to think that moon people (traditionally women) can show reason, reflection and objectivity from time to time.

RUSTY

Alchemy. It keeps presenting itself in relationship to Hermes, so perhaps the time has come for some digging and delving. Although it is her turn, Sandy says she feels faint at the mere thought of tackling this and besides, she points out, I am the one who is gung-ho on the subject. This is perfectly true. I once did a lot of work for a paper I decided to write in a moment of madness. At the time I knew nothing about Hermes, least of all his alchemical connection. Here is what I wrote:

> Alchemy is usually thought of as a consuming passion to transform base metals into gold and there is no doubt that the greedy, seduced by visions of fabulous wealth, converged upon the laboratory. Yet 'aurum nostrum non est aurum vulgi'—our gold is not common gold—was the constantly reiterated statement of the dedicated alchemist.
>
> Although alchemists unquestionably surrounded themselves with all the paraphernalia of chemistry, the transformation they sought was not primarily physical. To be sure, if by some marvelous happenstance a river of gold were to burst from a smoldering pot, there would be general rejoicing. There would be an equal—or possibly a greater—elation were matter suddenly to reveal the secret of its construction. Nonetheless the goal of the alchemist was not, in essence, material.

I think now I would add something to the effect that

fundamentally, the alchemist believed it should be possible both to materialize the spiritual and to spiritualize the material—what somebody lyrically called "divine bi-unity."

Hermes is very present in the alchemist's world, ambiguous like the unicorn, syncretic—in a word, androgynous. But dipping again into the realm of alchemy, I have come upon an unexpected denizen—the swan!

Swans, especially sacred to Aphrodite, stand for beauty. The swan's phallic neck is masculine, its shapely body feminine. Apollo's chariot, hauled across the daytime sky by a golden stallion, was returned across the moonlit night-time waters by a great, glimmering silvery swan. This general ambivalence intrigued the alchemists who, perceiving swans as androgynous, compared them to Mercury.

I was just about to fold my tent when Monsieur Cirlot gave me one more insight. He says that the pre-Copernicans saw the heavenly series Sun-Mercury-Moon as not only central in the heavens but of central importance to the human spirit. The sun is the zenith, the moon the nadir and Mercury the connecting center.

And here come the alchemists again. Because Mercury is nearest the sun, he is closely related to gold and since gold comes from the earth—and is in fact the image of the sun in the earth—Mercury has a double nature. This borders on the far-fetched, but who am I to criticize the ancients, particularly when they enhance the general gorgeousness of Hermes. Did you, or I, or almost anyone know that there exists something called the emblem of Hermes? No you didn't, but there is. It consists of the signs for sun and moon with the unlikely addition of a cross—unlikely until you discover that in antiquity the cross symbolized the connection between heavenly and earthly.

SANDY

Intrigued by all this planet business, I dug into a bit of stuff here and there and found something truly fascinating and, to me anyway, truly new as well.

In Cabalism, there are seven mirrors which correspond to the seven planets and should be consulted on the correct day, astrologically speaking.

The sun mirror (well, the sun isn't a planet, but let's not be picky) is made of gold and is to be consulted on Sundays as to great people presently on earth. On Mondays, the moon mirror is to be consulted as to dreams. The Mars mirror is iron and, consulted on Tuesdays, reveals data on enmities. The Mercury mirror is crystal filled with quicksilver and, on Wednesdays, has much to say about money. On Thursdays, the Jupiter mirror, made of tin, deals with probability—or at least possibility—of success. The mirror of Venus, gleaming copper, deals (as expected) with love—on Fridays. The lead Saturn mirror, if approached on a Saturday, may reveal the place of lost articles.

Should we take a leaden mirror on our trips?

RUSTY

I shall now quote from what has become almost my favorite book—and in a house containing some several thousand volumes, that's heavy praise.

I can't seem to remember where I came upon the spectacular book, *The Gods of Greece*, by the spectacular Arianna Stassinopoulos Huffington (Harry N. Abrams, Inc., 1989). The when is also vague, but it was published in the 1980s and entered our lives some time later. I know it was after we had at long last recognized Hermes, since I remember giving Sandy my copy in Boston. I left her to leaf through it alone because its impact is too marvelous to be diluted by another presence. Actually, in an ideal world the book should be universally required reading. Fat chance—so here are some bits and pieces, each (for me and surely for You-and-I) shining jewels:

> Only by celebrating the gods and being moved by them will we be able to rescue them from the hands of philologists and mythologists busy burying them under piles of scientific data. Nor is this an idle rescue operation. At a time when myth has become practically a synonym for falsehood...the Greek gods can guide us to forgotten dimensions of our lives and ourselves.
>
> No part of life was complete for the Greeks without the divine, and nothing was more natural than to be surrounded by gods and filled with them...The gods are so actively and naturally present in everyday life that holiness has no place in Greek religion. Miracles have no place in it either, or to put it another way, everything is a miracle.
>
> The gods roamed the earth, clad in hundreds of guises...Nothing important happens without the gods manifesting themselves, yet the natural course never seems interrupted...These divine interventions, far from being miraculous, are seen as the very essence of

everyday experience because the divine is seen as the basis of all being and reality.

The sanctifying of the everyday, one of the highest ideals of all religions, is here a living truth.

Stassinopoulos continues:

In Homer, the darkness and the light are not separate divinities but contained within each god. The gods who create are the gods who destroy. In dramatic contrast to the idea that has dominated Western culture of one great god and one great, contending principle of evil, each Greek god contains a polarity, an inner tension, a light and a dark side that casts a shadow variously shaped according to his particular character.

How about that for an example of androgyny? I'm panting in pursuit.

Man is as much in the image of the gods and goddesses, when he is creative, joyful, triumphant, as when his dark underside is showing.

The gods do not tell us how to live. They are neither moral nor immoral, neither teachers nor examples. They simply provide an invisible background against which our lives take on new meaning.

Greek gods mirror accurately, not wishfully, who we are. The Greek religion is not a religion of serene, perfected being but of tumultuous becoming: sensual, emotional, impulsive. It is significant that Homer places the gods not in heaven, in a psychological outer space, but on Olympos—on top of a mountain but still

> firmly attached to the earth. And the Greeks could both revere them and laugh with them; and the gods would laugh back.

Can you imagine Moses, Jesus or Mohammed being allowed a belly laugh—or even a joyous snort?

SANDY

How Melanie, I suddenly thought, would your grandmother and your great-aunt have fared in this shining Greek world? Would we have been citizens in history's first democracy? No. Would we have been free to seek, to stride fearlessly toward the light? Apparently not.

But this is strange, isn't it, since the Greek goddesses are just as powerful as the gods. Moreover, in the original pantheon there were six of each. Late in the game, the Olympians admitted Dionysus and Hades, which unbalanced things. And, as has often been pointed out, females got some of the very best parts in Greek mythology. The Fates and the Muses and Graces were women, and the deathless playwrights and sculptors of ancient Greece gave women a magnificent share in their creations. There were also the wild Maenads who, while hardly praiseworthy, were certainly conspicuous. It seems that the Greeks perceived females and males as equal on Olympos and in the hearts and minds of geniuses but not on the streets of Athens. How come?

I asked Rusty.

RUSTY

When I began pondering the position of human females in ancient Greece, I wandered far and hugely enjoyed myself. This is what I learned—or rather relearned, because this stuff is familiar to me in bits and pieces, but startling when put together.

From observing creatures of all kinds giving birth, it undoubtedly seemed clear to our remote ancestors that the feminine was of immense importance—that, in fact, Earth herself might be female. This, when you think of it, is reasonable, and a world where God could equally well be Goddess has become more and more accepted among modern anthropologists—not all of them of course. Rewriting prehistory (or any kind of history) is burdensome, but isn't it reasonable to assume that the earliest of our societies was motherly?

Did you think I was going to say matriarchal? Well, that's where I thought I was heading too—but not so. In *The Chalice and the Blade*, Riane Eisler remarks how logical it seems "that women would not be seen as subservient in societies that conceptualized the powers governing the universe in female form."

She adds that "effeminate" qualities such as caring, compassion and nonviolence would be highly valued in these societies.

"What does not make sense," she adds, "is to conclude that societies in which men did not dominate women were societies in which women dominated men."

Joseph Campbell agrees. I keep trying not to refer to him,

but what's the use? He is incomparable.

"In the early mythic systems," he points out, "divinity could be represented as well under feminine as under masculine form, the qualifying form itself being merely the mask of an ultimately unqualified principle beyond, yet inhabiting, all names and forms."

See where we're headed? But do not let me digress. From approximately 7500 B.C. to about 3500 B.C., communities that might be termed cooperative spread both leftward and rightward from their probable cradle in the Middle East. Then came the Aryan nomads from the north and the Semitic nomads from the south. And that was that.

Before their violent appearance, says Campbell, there had prevailed "an essentially organic, vegetal, non-heroic view of the nature and necessities of life that was completely repugnant to those lion hearts for whom...the battle spear and its plunder were the source of both wealth and joy."

Campbell continues:

> In the older mother myths and rites, the lighter and darker aspects of the mixed thing that is life had been honored equally and together, whereas in the later, male-oriented, patriarchal myths, all that is good and noble was attributed to the new, heroic master gods. Where the goddess had been venerated as the giver and support of life...women as her representative had been accorded a paramount position...Opposed to such without question is the order of Patriarchy, with its ardor of righteous eloquence and a fury of fire and sword.

And they've been at it ever since. Political and theological patriarchies ended up by taking over the world—not all at once, of course. It happened piecemeal, and is described most entertainingly by Campbell. Ancient epics, he tells us, can be schematized in four steps:

1) the world born of a goddess without consort;
2) the world born of a goddess fecundated by a consort;
3) the world fashioned from the body of a goddess by a male warrior-god;
4) the world created by the unaided power of a male god alone.

And now we come to Carolyn Heilbrun, whose book *Toward a Recognition of Androgyny* abruptly, and quite recently, entered my life. I knew about Heilbrun, but had never heard of this opus. It just appeared (friend-of-a-friend business), but you know what, or who, is really behind this kind of thing.

The good society, the only society that can possibly save us and our planet, states Heilbrun, is androgynous! For her, sexual polarization is a disaster. Like everyone else, she quotes Campbell, picking out for emphasis his feeling that the "patriarchal, anti-androgynous view is distinguished by its setting apart of all pairs of opposites—male and female, life and death, true and false, good and evil."

In an ideal (i.e. androgynous) society, a woman would be perceived as a person "before she was thought of as somebody's mother or wife or mistress, but in our present world only men are perceived first and foremost as persons."

Freud, of course, saw females of our species as indubitably inferior—also incomplete, lacking a penis for which they must always long. I've never known a woman who wanted a penis, and I've asked quite a few. Against Freudian views of life we must all, says Heilbrun, male and female alike, struggle hard and persistently: "The sexes require one another for civilization. Walls must be climbed together."

So what about Athens, which was my point of departure for all this? Well, here's the way I now see things:

By the time Great Greece burst upon history's horizon, the androgynous society no longer prevailed anywhere. The very last was Crete, and the ancient Cretans had bitten the dust seven hundred years before our story begins. A long time? Yes, but not long enough to erase all the past. Goddesses remained equal to gods in Greece and here and there in the east and west, though obviously not in the lands of the Old Testament. And it wasn't only female denizens of Olympos who were respected. In the arts of Greece, women stood very tall indeed.

But on the streets of Athens? No.

Now here is something intriguing. No, that's too small a word. Enthralling might be better. What we have here is the last—the very last—chapter in an androgynous drama of world-wide significance. Patriarchy had wiped out flesh-and-blood equality but the concept still held for other-worldly matters. If every last trace of androgyny had faded, Great Greece could not have endured long enough to perform the unique and everlasting miracles which have shaped every facet of the western world.

SANDY

Dazzling moonlight last night made me think of all the tales we have heard about how not just the dog but probably every animal reacts to the moon at its brightest.

Recently, a woman whose son is a policeman told me that constabularies dread a full moon because crime from the petty to the terminal increases when the moon is at its brightest. And the Christian fundamentalists are trying to persuade us that we are not related to any other creature, being made solely in the image of a sole deity whom they alone know!

And of course it's just this that leads to theological warfare. Rusty and I talk about this all the time. None of the ensuing horrors, the mayhem and mutilation, rapine and rape, result from the ins and outs of polytheism—certainly not Greek polytheism. You can't fight about it.

The Greeks, says our mutual friend Joseph Campbell,

> ...were proud of being the ones in the world to have learned at last how to live as men might live, not as servants...obedient to some conjured divine law, nor as the functionaries, trimmed to size, of some ever-wheeling cosmic order; but as rationally judging men, whose laws were voted on, not 'heard'; and consequently in whose sciences truth, not fancy, was at last actually beginning to appear. A discovered cosmic order was not read as a design for the human order, but as its frame and limitation.
>
> There was always destiny, which limits even the gods. The Greek view suggests an indefinable circum-

> scription, within the bounds of which both gods and men work their individual wills, ever in danger of violating the undefined bounds and being struck down, yet with play enough—within limits—to achieve a comely realization of ends humanly conceived.

It makes me want to dance about.

RUSTY

Religion. What is it?

"Religion," said the Star Island Scholars many years ago, when they were struggling with definitions at their Science and Religion conference, "is man's effort to orient himself in the universe."

Are we (You-and-I) experiencing a god's effort to come into dimension instead of a human effort to escape it? We never sought a god or made any attempt to discover a religion, much less create a theology. We were the sought, not the seekers; the pursued, not the pursuers. Clearly, the god was there first, not any desire on our part to discover or create him/her/it. There was no goal known to us. We just thought we were taking a series of trips, but they were not common-garden-variety trips and some kind of goal most certainly existed. As things now appear, we were on a pilgrimage peppered with revelations to which we were, for far too long, blind as bats. So all right, where are we?

The first thought that flaps up to the surface is this: the once-upon-a-time Greeks, most particularly those who lived in the fifth and fourth centuries B.C., were the wonders of the world. To be sure, they didn't start from nothing. For centuries, Mesopotamian and Egyptian minds had been busying themselves with the universal riddles that we're still scrabbling around with. But on those early bases the Greeks constructed intellectual towers and artistic gardens and lagoons which have never been surpassed.

History acknowledges this whole-heartedly. Our philosophies and politics, our sciences, our approach to the visual arts and to drama, poetry, games, history, and mathematics all spring from Greek roots. Explanations for this phenomenon go a little way, but always fail in the end. Even the soberest researchers tend to resort, however reluctantly, to the word miracle.

But when scholars, school teachers, librarians, tourists, you-name-it, get to Greek religion, they smile indulgently and use the word myth—not with understanding but patronizingly, as a synonym for fairy tale. Here are some definitions of myth I've collected from here and there. All definers are 20th Century.

Mary Midgley: "To call something a myth does not mean it is a false story. It means that it has great symbolic power which is independent of its truth."

J.B. Bierlien: "Myth does not mean falsehood, but rather a vehicle by which truth was conveyed."

Carl Jung: "Myths tells us in picture language of powers of the psyche to be recognized and integrated in our lives… They can never be displaced by the findings of science."

Pierre Janet: "Myths are a vehicle for truth, not an unquestioned truth in themselves."

Ananda Coomaraswamy: "Myth embodies the nearest approach to absolute truth that can be expressed in words."

Mercea Eliade: "Myth is the record of the breakthrough of the transcendent into our world."

This is not stuff to patronize! The Greeks, like everybody else, needed to orient themselves. Surely the only satisfactory way to pass judgement on any orientation is to see where it leads and/or has led. "By their fruits," in other words, "you shall know them." The ancient Greeks were polytheists. The Jews, Moslems and Christians are monotheists. By what fruit can we know them?

When I finally finished my world history, a lot of people asked me a certain question (well, not a lot really. Large clumps of former buddies gave me a wide berth. Members of polite society rarely sit down and write a world history).

The question, more or less, was "Can you at this point make any statement that applies to the whole story of man?" The answer is easy. He fights, mainly about land and theology.

Everybody fights about land—defending it, trying to steal it or trying to get it back when lost to tougher thieves or secessionists. Everybody struggles over territory. But only monotheists fight about theology. Enormous numbers of Jews, Moslems and Christians kill, torture and imprison one another (snatching territory en route) with persistent regularity. They have been at this for hundreds and hundreds of years and show no signs of stopping.

This comes about because if you have only one deity (always a he, of course. so you're already leaning toward the battlefield), then you've got to make him responsible for everything and in charge of everything, and you've got to say how. There is of course little agreement here, but you're not allowed to "agree to disagree," since their leaders assert that error has to be eliminated along with the erroneous believer.

Of course, come to think of it, even the monotheisms have trouble putting everything in one pair of hands. If a deity is omnipotent, omniscient and benevolent (at least to his followers), then how account for evil?

You can't, so you have two choices. Either you introduce a Bad Guy, which makes your unadulterated monotheism look shaky, or you put the blame on the highest form of life, which is manifestly unfair since if I was made by this omnipotent, omniscient and benevolent deity, who is at fault for my deplorable behavior and rotten school spirit?

When any of us determinedly concentrate our minds on theology, it's not hard to grasp the fact that all theologies begin the same way. We turn religious—we make an effort to orient ourselves in the universe.

The first observation we make is that we're scared. We need a lot more power than we're likely to find here on earth, so we must search elsewhere for powerful allies. But the problem here is that when we find allies that are suitably frightening, they frighten us, too. Judaism, Christianity and Islam are scary. To be sure, some Jews, Christians and Moslems are more scared than others, but one all-powerful God to whom we belong body and soul but who is fundamentally unknown, unknowable and tricky to please is hardly a basis for peace of mind, let alone a cause for rejoicing. The same uncertainties are true of most oriental theologies—complex systems rife with crowds of divinities who may or may not be on your team at any given moment.

Then there is the question of founders. All the monotheisms have founders. Except the most recent (Mohammed), these founders have become gods, demi-gods or, in the case of Christianity, the One God Himself.

But when the Greeks took up the task of orienting themselves in their universe, they did something different. They did not work downwards from Unknowable Powers but upward from where they stood. It seemed clear to them that the forces which sway us, making us act as we do, are real. They exist. They are there. Moreover, they are universal—prevailing, in other words, everywhere. In their efforts to express this striking insight, the Greeks found themselves more and more captivated by the concept of personification.

The gods who evolved were not mysteries. They were real personages, with real strengths and weaknesses. They can be understood. They are neither monstrous like the deities of pre-Greek antiquity, nor remote like the Lord of the monotheists. They are formed in the image of Greeks—or Greeks are formed in their image. It doesn't really matter how you phrase it.

The Greeks came to see their gods, says Campbell, as

> …aspects of the universe—children of chaos and the great Earth, just as men are. And even chaos and the great Earth produced our world not through acts of creative will, but as seeds produce trees, out of the natural spontaneity of their substance. The secret of this spontaneity may be learned or sensed in silence, in the mysteries and throughout life, but it is not definable as the will, work or divine plan of a personality. So at no time in the history of properly Greek thought does the idea appear of a book of moral statutes revealed…from a sphere antecedent to and beyond the laws of nature.

In the doings of their gods, the Greeks saw vivid reflections of their own puzzles and failures, successes and delights. In such a setting, human life gained clarity, significance, above all value.

To the poet Auden, belief in Ares or Aphrodite meant simply that "the poetic myths about them do justice to the forces of sex and aggression as human beings experience them in nature and their own lives."

So far as I can see, Greek theology really does stand alone, the only one with which someone like me can identify. It is vivid, joyous, fearless, personal—above all, accessible.

According to Campbell, when the Greeks "kissed their fingers at the moon, or at rosy-fingered dawn, they did not fall on their faces but approached it man to man or man to goddess—and what they found was already what we have found: that all is indeed wonderful, yet submissive to examination."

The Greek answer to the Great Question is central to the particular wonders of Greek creativity from which all our arts and sciences spring. Anyone traveling to Greece and then to Egypt can instantly grasp the astonishing difference between ancient cultures. Greece brings gods and humans together, raising us up to show how high we can go. In Egypt we are reduced, crushed, inconsequential.

The miracle of Greece is an endlessly reiterated statement. Well, I don't mind coming right out with the answer even if the learned scholars always present themselves as baffled. The miracle of Greece, the marvelous creativity from which all our arts and sciences spring, is centered in a particular form of polytheism.

I got out my Edith Hamilton books, which I haven't

perused for years.

The Greeks banished a world filled with the irrational, she says. "Astronomy, not astrology, is what the Greek mind made of the stars."

Frightening priests who can influence gods are absent. In *The Odyssey*, she reminds us, when a priest and a poet, trembling before Odysseus, beg him to spare their lives, the hero slays the priest but saves the poet. He was, Hamilton explains, unable to slay "a man who had been taught his divine art by the gods. Not the priest but the poet had influence with heaven."

And, she adds, "no one was ever afraid of a poet. Ghosts, too, which have played so large and so fearsome a part in other lands, never appear on earth in any Greek story." The Greeks, you see, were not afraid of the dead.

Imagine! How can anyone believe our way of dealing with Ultimate Things is superior. We are terrified of the dead.

It is important to remember that not all the tales of godly derring-do are significant. Some are simply entertainment—early forms of make-believe told in a dawning literary age. On this score, Hamilton makes a significant and totally charming comment.

Even the most nonsensical, we read, "takes place in a world which is essentially rational...The winged steed Pegasus, after skimming the air all day, went every night to a comfortable stable in Corinth."

Bliss!

But Hamilton is troubled by the dark spots in the picture. She is not happy that the behavior of the gods frequently offends decency. But that is just the point! The Greek gods behave the way we behave when we're indecent as well as decent. When we see our faults and failings right out in plain sight we contemplate them, and in so doing, perhaps we change. At least that's the way the Greeks seem to have seen it.

Chapter 2

SANDY

We had surely been assured by the overwhelming Bermuda trip that the next chapter of You-and-I would be one of the most important parts of our unfolding pilgrimage.

Then why in the world go back to New Orleans? Why be obsessed to return after that first ghastly trip? Why, indeed—but we were. Another trip to New Orleans, while miserable to contemplate, was impossible to ignore. Maybe some sense could be made of that hateful jumble. We would carefully respond to any clue or symbol.

We saw to it that reservations were confirmed in a respectable and comfortable bed and breakfast.

I arrived first in Atlanta, where Rusty was to meet me. As we sat waiting for the departure of the plane to New Orleans, two middle-aged, unremarkable ladies went by, both dressed in most remarkable flame-colored dresses. They were not orange, not red, but flame—there was no other word for it. It was a heavenly color, but it consumed the middle-aged ladies.

The plane trip was uneventful. No flames, thank heaven, but a thunder of the usual uncontrollable sneezing, not ker-choos but paroxysms, violent and loud. I have always loved sneezing, not only because it feels wonderful but because it is just about the only activity you cannot be blamed for. It's loud, unexpected, rude, out of control and unattractive, yet a sneezer is never socially scorned.

We arrived and loved our bed and breakfast. Again, we went up a flight of stairs to a balcony as at North Rampart Street, but the steps were shiny and the balcony overlooked a lovely garden of trees, shrubs and flowers.

The room was rectangular, with a moss green carpet and a wall of glass. There were good beds, two desks, lots of light and lots of hangers. The bathroom had a functional stopper in the tub, a shower cap, terry robes and a telephone. This telephone, as well as the one in the bedroom, actually connected with the world and brought us breakfast each morning. Also, the curtains and bedspreads matched and were flame colored.

The following day, after a breakfast in bed of rich coffee and biscuits with honey, we went out with the old, undaunted expectation and excitement.

What a wonderful day! The streets and stores were happy and welcoming, and Royal Street was dancing with old-fashioned jugglers, mimes and music and many of our symbols from past years. What a dazzle of unicorns, sneezes, owls, pussy cats, turkeys, carousels, rainbows, and moons!

Also, there were people on the street and in the restaurants who were gaspingly like people we loved in those days. Everyone turned to us. At lunch, the waitress hugged me when she brought the wrong order. A marvelous man with a pink face and white beard blew a kiss and played Dixieland music.

"You are a very old soul," an immobile mime suddenly announced to Rusty.

Then, after being embraced and reassured and filled with bliss, after reliving the wondrous past, we were astounded by insistent new symbols.

It started in a store full of swords, flintlocks and coins. Swords and flintlocks are not in any way our delight. But the coins? For no reason, we each bought a Piece of Eight and thought of Long John Silver, whose parrot said, "Pieces of eight, pieces of eight."

From then on, parrots were everywhere. Red parrots and green parrots, parrots on stands in the street, parrots on people's shoulders, real parrots, stuffed parrots. Next were keys—clumsy, pirate trunk keys, small silver jewel-box keys. We each bought crossed brass keys enclosed in a brass circle.

Then the number four. Everywhere were metal fours, wooden fours, paper fours. The number four jumped out of show cases and the leaves of books.

Finally, with the help of a book of symbols in the public library, we began to understand. Subsequently pondering the matter, we decided that no trip before or since had proved so lavish with Signs of Otherness.

PARROTS: symbols of the limitation of words...words

in a parrot's chatter are probably without meaning. Words are not the only, or even the best means of communication. Hermes has never used words with us.

THE NUMBER FOUR is heavy with meaning: the ages of the world—gold, silver, bronze, iron. Points of the compass. Winds. Limbs. And four is one of the symbols of Hermes.

KEYS: talismans worn for remembrance of things past. That which solves the unintelligible. That which prepares or opens a way to other objects and further progress. Authority and super consciousness. Crossed keys in a yellow circle are knowledge and love surrounded by power and authority!

SNEEZES: among the Greeks, a good omen of heavenly origin!

FLAME: life force, wisdom. That which is always active, never still. In some parts of the ancient world flames symbolized those who had successfully endured the grossness of the corporeal world and so were released into souls. Fluttering flames and fluttering butterflies are interchangeable (we are frequently surrounded by butterflies, real and fake).

Here is what Jung had to say: "Who speaks in primordial images speaks to us as with a thousand trumpets. He grips and overpowers, and at the same time he elevates that which he treats out of the individual and transitory into the sphere of the eternal."

***

One morning, dizzy with excitement, we sat blissfully eating biscuits and honey. I told Rusty about a new method of meditation that I had just heard of. We had tried and tried to meditate and both had taken courses in transcendental meditation. It seemed such an obvious way of communication. But never had it been successful and we were frustrated.

This morning, however, interested in anything and everything, we started calling for information. No luck at first, but eventually we connected with Yogi Ralph of Crystal Accents. How could Yogi Ralph remain unexplored?

A cab took us to one of the far borders of the city. Yogi Ralph's house was enchanting and so was Yogi Ralph. He was young, red-headed and terribly sincere. We had a marvelous hour with him staring into a candle flame. Nothing happened to me, and I don't know about Yogi Ralph, but Rusty, who almost never cries, momentarily burst into tears and then just as suddenly grew cheery again.

We left this charming man with a happy feeling of closeness and a strong desire to explore this further. I remember that we all three hugged and Yogi Ralph gave each of us a flame red jasper stone.

The next day we bought tall sticks and candles and we diligently tried (then and later) to meditate, but it just isn't our vehicle of communication. Once again it was clearly shown to us that Hermes waits not upon established patterns—nor is it ever our deal. This was the last message of this wondrous trip.

"But it's just a reminder," Rusty protested. "We've never been in command. *Custody* is what we've been in—always and right from the start."

When we began to think about it, we not only saw that this was true but that a whole lot of other situations had existed from the beginning—even from the very day we met. Here they are:

TIME: Everyday time, as measured in everyday life, ceases to function. It expands. It contracts. It appears to adjust to us. The exact amount—an hour, a day, a week—is allotted us to complete each happening. (Each scene? Each instruction? Each disclosure?)

TRAVEL: We take to the road—always. At the very start we dubbed our adventures *trips*—long before we grasped the multiple meanings: a physical excursion; a hallucinogenic excursion; a slip; a nimble step; to set free by releasing a catch; to break out an anchor by lifting or turning over.

PRICE: It is never considered. We have, from the onset, had an inchoate sense that it will not be higher than we can pay.

PATTERNS: Ordinary patterns of living are blurred or absent. On the other hand, our trips are clearly and strongly patterned.

STORES: Many of our messages are received through the medium of stores—and this leads on to

PUNS: They surround us like a nimbus. For example: something is *in store* for us; we have very high regard for what befalls us, i.e. we set great *store* by our happenings; we know that things are *stored* up for our future; that which has already befallen us is *stored* in our memory banks. And remember the mist-missed embroglio?

We didn't have enough trip hours left to do any delving into the matter of puns, so when we got home we pooled bits and pieces of research and came up with the following: "The use of a word or combination of words so as to emphasize different meanings or applications, or the use of words that are alike or nearly alike in sound but different in meaning; a play on words, producing an odd effect."

That's what the dictionary has to say. Now hear from the Thesaurus. (A thesaurus, by the way, is a treasury, or *storehouse*.)

A PUN dwells among

1) Similarities where it rubs shoulders with counterparts and second selves;

2) Absurdities where it associates with paradox, extravagance & improvisation;

3) Ambiguities where it keeps company with oracles, conundrums and double entendres;

4) Witticisms where it skips about among shenanigans, jests, quips and harlequinades.

Well, you hardly have to puzzle any more as to why Hermes and puns seem so persistently connected! I hope, Melanie, that you haven't turned into one of those people who automatically (and for unknown reasons) groans when puns appear. Not only are they clever in their own right but obviously very dear to the heart of Hermes—and with the heart of Hermes you don't play fast and loose.

RUSTY

"How would you define our relationship to one another?" I asked Sandy on one of our trips.

"Do we have to?" she muttered, removing her shoes, belt and dark glasses after an extensive urban exploration.

"Well, of course we don't *have* to," I replied, picking up my novel.

"I see what you mean," she remarked brightly, awakening from a nap which she regularly claims not to have taken.

"So let's."

We undertook the project while the shadows lengthened. Certainly the relationship is intimate. Just as certain, it's not sexual—and that's as far as we got.

On the way to dinner we passed a toy store window all decked out with African animals except for a kangaroo right in the middle. This was obviously a Hermes comment, so we repaired to the library, which was closed along with the stores.

Frustration drove us to call my daughter who, although in the middle of a party and lacking in enthusiasm, looked up kangaroo in a dictionary of symbols. "Symbolic of boon companionship," she informed us.

How, I asked Sandy, would you define a boon companion? We agreed that we were totally familiar with and to each other and, suddenly, with a whoop, we saw possibilities not so much in the adjective as in the noun familiar. Early the next morning we set sail to do our research.

"The idea underlying the familiar," announces the dusty F volume of an ancient encyclopedia "is the notion of angelus or genius, guardian spirits."

How totally delightful and unexpected! It appears that familiars can be any kind of creature including homo sapiens. That's what we are, then. We're one another's familiars.

We did not pick each other out. We were chosen for an adventure. We do not face each other, but rather stand shoulder to shoulder, looking outward—close but not touching—enveloped by what the physicists call a force field. And a force field is "a region or space under the influence of some agent!"

Chapter 3

SANDY

Of course, after the Great Revelation we suspected that since Hermes had been speaking to us for many decades in the language of symbolism, he would probably continue to do so, whenever and wherever we went.

Sure enough. On a trip to New York, our eyes on stems and our ears quivering, we walked block after block down, block after block up. At the door of a large church on upper Fifth Avenue I said, "Let's go in."

"Why?"

"Just let's." So we did.

There was a vestibule entirely papered with fleur-de-lis. This seemed as inexplicable as my odd compulsion—so we knew that once more we were being addressed. Unable to face the New York Public library, we repaired to a bookshop and made for the nearest dictionary/encyclopedia section. (We do this from time to time and buy a book when guilt—or hostile stares from the owner—compels us.)

FLEUR DE LYS: a mythical bloom, literally flower-of-the-lily, but sometimes translated as flower-of-light. A triad representing the masculine principle ringed by the female. Its three petal form closely resembles an iris tied by an encircling band.

TRIAD: a group of three closely associated persons.

IRIS: a beautiful female messenger of the gods who travels on rainbows.

We wobbled back to our hotel and over tea cups gawked at one another. As usual we knew the objects presented to us but nothing—absolutely nothing—about their symbolism. That it was a message from Hermes was obviously not in doubt.

"We couldn't have made this up, could we?"

"Of course not. We don't know anything about any of this."

We have this conversation over and over again.

RUSTY

The harlequin came to occupy a large space in our You-and-I lives (by now, Melanie, I assume you are more or less shock-proof and able to shrug and accept peculiar sentences).

He first claimed our attention in Montreal in the usual way, his image springing up everywhere. Since the appearance of

Hermes, we regularly assumed that all symbols would prove a message from him—and so they did, but never, never in any way that could have been anticipated. As usual, we left ultimate meanings to present themselves in their own good time, and set forth to do some shopping

Since wands and harlequins seemed to be inseparable, we went on a wand hunt—something, we thought, from a fairy-tale, long and delicate. Cold trail. Finally, just as we were about to give up, at least for that day, we saw a robust china harlequin wielding a completely different kind of wand, something sturdy like a scepter or staff—something, in fact, such as Hermes might carry, though we didn't catch this at first. Well, these progressions of ideas aren't easy.

All evening we pondered, arriving finally at the thought that the kind of stakes that held up banisters would probably be the closest approximation to what a harlequin would carry. In the phone book we found a furniture outlet that sold "Absolutely Everything You Might Need."

Since we were in Montreal, addresses meant nothing. We just hailed a taxi and set off—and off and off and off. Finally clearly outside the city and facing an astronomic meter debt, we arrived not at a furniture outlet but a vast furniture factory. A salesman presently appeared.

"You want two what?"

We explained to him what we wanted.

"You drove all the way out here for two sticks?"

"Well, it would be nice if they were carved a little."

Muttering, he led us through the factory, pointed to a beautiful pile of what were obviously harlequin wands, and disappeared. We chose two, left a little note (with a little cash) and returned to Montreal. When we had summoned the hotel carpenter to remove four inches off the ends and bought a little oil to stain them, we had two perfect, and obviously magic, wands. We have never since gone on a trip without them.

But a number of messages lodged in the harlequin and were presently revealed. Instead of the trip we had planned a few months later, I helped Sandy move. Hermes, however, was not put out (though we were). In the first bookstore I entered upon my return home, I was compelled to buy a book called *The Triumph of Pierrot: The Commedia dell' Arte and the Modern Imagination*, by two writers named Martin Green and John Swan.

"I knew nothing about this book—had never even heard of it," I wrote Sandy. "But the more I read, the more persuaded I became that Hermes gave us what he had in mind for this meeting by making me buy and study this strange book."

Here are some random thoughts I gleaned:

The chief characters in the world of the *Commedia* are Pierrot and Harlequin. Pierrot is a mysterious, poetic figure linked to the moon, usually masked, (masks are among our most persistent symbols), suggesting magic, secrecy and ambiguity.

Harlequin is a chameleon. Agile and mercurial, he can assume any role he chooses. By and large he skirts or ignores the law but is never caught, never judged, never punished. All communication is in pantomime and is always unexpected. Though the dominant figure is Harlequin, roles can change and "even the great Harlequin, Picasso," seems on occasion to have "detected a Pierrot in himself." Sandy and I are obsessed by Picasso! Truly.

Everyone involved with Pierrot/Harlequin is a wanderer. Also, insofar as possible, there is a complete denial of gender.

"Some Harlequins match the splendor of the women whom they resemble. Placed at the frontiers of life, animals are human, and the sexes indistinct." In the magical world of *Commedia* there is a combination of "the grandly traditional with the irreverently experimental and the religiously noble with the morally absurd." And there is always a marvelous mixture of "esoteric mysticism and cabaret gaiety."

If this seems Hermes-ish to you, Melanie, you're RIGHT ON. After reading this book, I had the feeling that Harlequin, Hermes and Picasso were practically interchangeable. The authors agree.

"The preference that Picasso shows for Harlequin," he writes, "suggests that analogies must exist between him and this legendary character."

And that's not all. It seems that the poet Apollinaire used to call his friend Picasso "Harlequin Trismegistus"—substituting the name Harlequin for Hermes!

If Sandy were here, she would ask quaveringly, "Is this possible?"

And I would reply "No, but it *happened*—all of it, the whole thing."

SANDY

When reading and rereading Rusty's section about the strange book that came into her hands recently, I concentrated, obviously, on the characters of Pierrot and Harlequin.

However, something kept niggling at me and I realized that it was Green and Swan's quotation, "Placed at the frontiers of life, animals are human and the sexes are indistinct."

I know they weren't referring to animals that sit up and beg and do human tricks. I feel sure I do know what they meant—the overwhelming recognition that all creatures have a deep common bond.

As you know, Melanie, I live surrounded by animals—some wild and some I have rescued. Each creature lives here in basic companionship, free to come and go in the woods and marshes.

On the island there are more than one thousand wild pigs descended, it is thought, from pigs brought here by the Spanish explorers when they first arrived in the new world. They are wiry, fast and self sufficient as they exist in the thirty odd thousand acres of near wilderness.

Lucky was brought to me when he was a few weeks old. A hawk had plunged down through the trees, grabbed this piglet and was carrying him away. He was not more than ten inches long. Thanks be, a friend witnessed this, shot a gun in the air, frightened the hawk who dropped the piglet.

I tended his wounds and brought him up on a bottle.

He was named Lucky for obvious reasons. Lucky lived in the house most of the time, went for long walks with me and drove with me to the beach to dig for small crabs and wade in pools. Today, because of handouts when I feed the horses, geese and peacocks, he weighs more than two hundred pounds. He loves everyone and is famous up and down the coast.

Lucky's dear and abiding love is a Paso Fino stallion

named Poco. Lucky used to follow Poco everywhere. When we went riding, he would follow as far as he could then wait until we returned and follow us home. He was with the horses all the time, even sleeping with them.

Alas, Poco belongs to the island manager, and one day it was decided that the manager's horses were to be moved to the mainland. All of us went through a period of panic and despair, but the day came. Lucky followed the trailer that took Poco to the dock where the barge was anchored, waiting to carry the horses across the water. Lucky followed for two miles and when the trailer was loaded, he jumped after it to the deck of the barge.

We were aghast. When we tried to move him, this 200-pound pig jumped from the barge into a small boat tied to the floating dock and, by a miracle, from the small boat to the float and then back up on the big dock.

He stood on the end of the dock and watched the barge until it was out of sight. It was possible, we knew, that he would jump in the water and be drowned, but nothing could move him—pushing, pulling, prayers or corn. He stayed there all night.

The next morning he was back at the barn, but it was a long time before he was his own loving self and now he never follows the remaining horses.

Over the years I have come to believe that one of my missions is to save animals—orphans, strays, abandoned dogs, cats, birds, even horses and donkeys. Being alone a great deal, I usually form a natural relationship with them of one sort or another. This is understandable, but once I was told by an overnight guest that he had been part of a scene he would never forget.

I have a beloved little mix of a dog I had saved from a doomed litter of puppies in a nearby kennel. She has lived with me for ten years and is totally obsessed with retrieving sticks. Every guest is besieged until he plays with her.

The day of his visit, my friend was thus engaged out by the barn. He had become understandably bored and automatic when he happened to look up, focus on what he was doing, and saw that his stick was being brought back to him by a wild turkey. For several weeks, I had noticed a wild hen turkey watching when I fed the horses and played with my dog. My friend hesitates to talk about the day he played stick with a wild turkey.

I have five geese that were rescued from a pond on an abandoned farm. I have had them for years and they follow me everywhere, even into the kitchen. One big, white gander and I are particular friends.

One morning in January I woke to see everything covered with snow. A snowstorm on the coast of Georgia is very rare, and never has there been one in the lifespan of my geese.

The geese, peacocks and ducks were riveted. None dared to venture a step. Finally, my gander rose up to fly to more familiar ground, but there was none, which forced him to come down on an icy strip where he broke his leg.

I took him to a special veterinarian in town who put a pin in his leg. My instructions were to keep him in a confined space for three weeks. I was to give him a blue antibiotic pill every day as infection could be fatal.

I put him in a horse trailer with hay and water and each day presented a bowl of corn with a blue pill in it. For several days I watched the pill go down with the corn but that was it. Presently, he refused to swallow any medicine. There was always a pill in the bottom of his empty bowl or put to one side. I was worried about infection.

In desperation, the solution came to me. I dipped the blue pill in damp corn meal to disguise the color and the taste. I couldn't tell it from the corn and nor, obviously, could he. For the remaining weeks of recovery, the bowl was empty.

At last the leg was strong and my big white gander marched out of the trailer—good as new.

Later, happily, I jumped into the trailer to give it a good cleaning. In the farthest dark corner, I found a pile of blue pills with a coating of moldy corn meal.

RUSTY

And then along came the flamingo. Well, actually, this was a symbol that entered our lives in the distant past of You-and-I, but of course way back when we didn't see it as such.

When we were young, Sandy used to have fits of guilt because she was having such a wondrous time You-and-I-ing that she tended to forget her family for clumps of time (a real but indestructible absurdity because she is a first class mother). She associated this guilt with flamingos because at a moment of peak guilt—in a restaurant of all places—she looked at the wall frescoes and beheld flamingos surrounded by baby flamingos. This made her feel so faint that we had to leave the restaurant. Well, calm and balance while on a You-and-I adventure were not always easy to achieve.

The flamingo has pursued us all these years, at least sporadically, but it never seemed to have anything to do with

You-and-I until 1989, when we went to Washington to march for abortion rights.

It never occurred to us that anything You-and-I-ish would befall us on this very serious occasion, but before the march we went for a stroll and on the wall of an old building were carved the words *Plus Ultra!* In we went to ask why and whence, but of course nobody knew. It was, however, a nudge from you-know-who, and we were watchful.

We stayed at an old hotel where our room sported a bookcase with an ancient edition of the *World Book of Knowledge*. Just for the hell of it we decided (or more likely it was decided for us) to look up flamingo. We made two discoveries: one, that it is a bird that lays only one egg, a birth control symbol par excellence; and two, that it has a family all to itself—in other words, is a unique creature.

We also discovered (in a bookstore) that the flamingo is assumed to be the phoenix! Flamingo merely refers to the color. Its formal name is Phoenicopterus.

On a subsequent excursion, the curtain rose all the way. Waltzing off to the nearest public library to look up something entirely different, we found a brand new Time-Life book on alchemy which stated with no ifs, ands or buts, "the phoenix is the bird of Hermes." We also discovered that in China the phoenix is not only greatly revered but bears the name of *feng huang*, which means male-female!

SANDY

There's no use wondering why we go to this place rather than that place. Names just appear and we go. Hermes is the travel agent, not You-and-I.

So we went to Sanibel Island, and en route we talked about parrots. We had tried to add new stuff to what we already knew and had been drawn rather far afield. Here is something Rusty gleaned from the Upanishads:

> You are the dark-blue bird and the parrot with red
> eyes,
> You have the lightning as your child,
> You are the seasons and the seas
> Having no beginning, you abide with
> all-pervadingness
> Wherefrom all beings are born.

Campbell says that this refers to the following:

> Whoever thus knows "I am the imperishable" becomes the universal, and not even the gods can prevent him from becoming so, for he becomes thereby their very self. Hence, whoever worships another divinity thinking "He is one and I am another"—he knows not.
>
> This is not pleasing to Yahweh. Nor is it pleasing to those who worship any god. For according to this view, not any envisioned deity but the individual in his own reality is that which is the reality of being.

This is marvelous—and exciting. We certainly don't worship Hermes. He is part of us—or we're part of him. Rusty read all this stuff to me over cocktails—probably loud and clear enough to carry far afield. We're used to being stared at, but it may not all be benign admiration.

And did we find the dark-blue bird and the parrot with red eyes? Of course—but the parrot first. He was bright green and he sat on a perch in the entrance hall of some kind of public building. If anyone reading this wonders why a parrot should be in such a place, so did we, but only mildly. I don't even have an explanation of why Sandy and Rusty arrived in a public building in Sanibel. The thing is, you see, we're used to this kind of thing.

The dark-blue bird came along next. We only found him because I walked up to an official-looking person and asked, "Do you know of any dark-blue birds in the neighborhood?"

Rusty thought that for once this was a bit much, but there was no problem at all.

"Why, yes," he said casually. "In the trailer park over there—about halfway down on the right."

Sure enough, there he was—a big dark-blue bird in a big cage outside a shabby trailer. He looked like a mynah—sort of, anyway. He was handsome, with bright yellow eyes.

"Could you tell us about this bird?" we asked some children pitching horseshoes.

"Nope."

"Does he belong to you?"

"Nope. Belongs to Pop, but he ain't here."

End of story.

After the trip, I wrote to an ornithologist friend who wrote back as follows.

> Your mystery birds may remain mysteries without some more information, but I'm happy to take a stab at identifying them.

1.) The mynah is probably the Greater Hill Mynah, which is deep blue-black with yellow eyes and some bare yellow skin patches on the face. If you are not sure it was a mynah, several species of Old World Starlings (close relatives of the mynahs) have glossy, near-black plumage and bright yellow eyes with no bare skin on the face (e.g. Glossy Starling, Superb Starling).

2.) The parrot sounds like an Amazon-type parrot, basically green with occasional flashes of color in tail, wings and sometimes on the forehead, usually with yellow-orange eyes that turn orange-red as they age. These are only in Latin America, but lots have escaped in Miami and southern California.

RUSTY

One fine day we were ordered to go to Santa Fe, but before we left I had a long and very vivid dream. The main characters were a retired professor and his wife, the head of a large and successful arts center. We know them only medium-well, but dreams have their own rules, and in any case, the dream was not for them but for You-and-I. Upon awakening, I sat right down and sent them the following epistle.

Dear _______,

It seems that I am somehow involved with your purchase of a Cessna. (Awake, I know nothing about this word and had to ask Beek at breakfast.) The plane, which seats four, arrived last night on the beach of a lonely island off the coast of Georgia inhabited by my closest friend and erstwhile sister-in-law. The beach is spectacular—fifteen miles of hard, white sand—a good place, I suppose, to land a plane, though I don't know whether one ever was landed before this episode.

You may think you were in bed asleep last night but you (or at least your astral bodies) were on that beach with me and my sister-in-law. There were two other persons. The first was a small boy about whom I know nothing and who played only a small part in the episode and the second was the pilot. The latter is clear to me and I could draw his portrait if I could draw. He had swarthy, reddish-brown skin, very straight, very thick, black hair and a heavy flying jacket which he refused to remove despite a temperature in the high seventies. He spoke only in grunts and at first I thought he might be a mute, but now I am convinced he was an Amerind.

It seemed that I had to go over the plane to check that all was in readiness for you. This I did, but since I know almost nothing about planes and nothing whatsoever about aerodynamics, I give you fair warning. At this juncture, the small boy got a fishing rod and started to cast into the surf. He cast very badly and my sister-in-law begged me to take the rod from him and show him how to cast properly. Now this is odd because I loathe fishing. My poor grandfather who owned a beautiful fishing camp in the Catskills knocked himself out in my infancy trying to make fishing attractive—but to no avail. I even overheard him one evening saying to my father, "What in God's name is wrong with that girl?"

Anyway, last night I did as I was bid and, removing the rod from the boy, started casting. Instantly, I felt a tug and with the greatest difficulty hauled in a cobalt blue fish. Although only about ten inches long, the creature's weight was such that I could not hold on and yelled for help. You two and my s.i.l. and the pilot and the small boy all came racing to my assistance. It took three to hold my catch and three to get the hook out of its mouth, but we finally succeeded. This scene was tense because we all knew that it was essential to get that fish back in the water. The scene ended with all arms stretched out seaward—gracefully like a ballet act—while the fish gave a leap into the air and then disappeared.

Someday I would very much like to see the plane again, (though I really don't want to go up in it), so do call me some day to take a look at it. Oh, and since I'm not sure whether or not you really studied it on the beach, it is bone colored and decorated in orange.

Love to you both -

This was only the beginning.

The morning after Sandy and I arrived in Santa Fe, we saw (and I purchased) an extraordinary object made by one of the Pueblo Indians. It is an impressionistic, cream-colored plane with orange splotches and it's driven by a robust, red pilot. Four figures accrue to the plane which upon closer inspection turns out to be a fish with a blue tail. The pilots and associates have horns.

When we went to the marvelous Museum of International Folk Art, we discovered that the plane is a Day of the

Dead object. At the same place we learned that a blue fish is a noteworthy oriental symbol, one of its associations being celebrations, such as birthdays, of small boys!

The museum is filled with popular toys made specifically for the Day of the Dead as it is celebrated in Mexico. Miniature skulls and skeletons are available in all kinds of materials. There are miniature funeral processions, masked dolls and jumping jacks that leap out of coffins. And there are lots of sugar goodies to make things even happier. All of this, of course, is meant to introduce death as cheerfully as possible. A museum brochure quotes Octavio Paz with these words from his *Labyrinth of Solitude*:

> The word death is not pronounced in New York, Paris or London, because it burns the lips. The Mexican, in contrast, is familiar with death, jokes about it, caresses it, sleeps with it, celebrates it: it is one of his favorite toys and his most steadfast love. True, there is perhaps as much fear in his attitude as that of theirs, but at least death is not hidden away: he looks at it face to face, with impatience, disdain or irony.

Hermes the Divine Psychopomp, of course, loomed over the whole place. This would have been enough to captivate us thoroughly and permanently, but the trip was not over. We bought books about history and art and devoured them and then we came upon Paul Radin's *The Trickster: A Study in American Indian Mythology* (Schochem Books, 1972)—and bought no more.

The Trickster, Radin tells us, is not only the oldest figure in American Indian mythology, but probably in all mythologies. In some tribes he is looked upon as a full deity, even involved with the creation of the world. In others, he is connected to the deities but not quite a thoroughbred.

The problem was always the trickiness which made it difficult to elevate him or, if elevated, to keep him there. His sudden bursts of raucous mirth and his let's-turn-everything-upside-down made the proper solemnity hard to maintain. Three traits are always present whether the Trickster is a god, a demigod or both: He is always hungry, he is always in motion and he is always sexy. But even this is a more-or-less situation. His hunger is not necessarily just for physical food, his motion can be travel as well as restlessness and his sex, though most of the time conspicuously phallic, can abruptly become female if a big enough shock is in order.

One charming tale of Trickster was told by the Oglala Indians. There is no question here of any half-and-half. He is a full god but has to be punished for bringing ridicule on his associates. The penalty is banishment to the world of men where he will have no friends.

To this, writes Radin, "he is represented as responding with a long and loud laugh and as telling the supreme deity that he had forgotten the birds and the other animals; that he would dwell with them and talk with each in its own language; and that on earth he would enjoy himself."

Furthermore, when he wished to, or when the occasion warranted, he would make fools of mankind. Radin continues:

> The symbol which Trickster embodies is not a static one. It contains within itself the promise of differentiation, the promise of god and man. For this

> reason every generation occupies itself with interpreting Trickster anew. No generation understands him fully but no generation can do without him. Each had to include him in all its theologies, in all its cosmogonies, despite the fact that it realized he did not fit properly into any of them, for he represents not only the undifferentiated and distant past, but likewise the undifferentiated present within every individual. This constitutes his universal and persistent attraction. And so he became and remained everything to every man—god, animal, human being, hero, buffoon, he who was before good and evil, denier, affirmer, destroyer and creator. If we laugh at him, he grins at us. What happens to him happens to us.

Incidentally, Radin is not hung up on the human shape alone. The Trickster of the insect world, he tells us, is the spider; of the animal world, the coyote. Just the other day, I learned that, among many Indians, coyotes are known as God's Dogs.

At the back of Radin's book are some fascinating comments by Jung. He speaks of orgies in the medieval church, particularly those on the election of the Fools' Pope. Here, wrote a shocked observer "in the very midst of divine service, masqueraders with grotesque faces, disguised as women, lions, mummers, performed their dances." They also sang off-color ditties, parked their greasy picnics on the altar in the middle of mass, rattled dice, burned incense made of old shoe leather, and skipped about all over the church.

So popular were these cheerful orgies that it took the church centuries to stamp them out. They demonstrate, wrote Jung, "the role of the trickster to perfection and when they vanished from the precincts of the church, they appeared again on the profane level of Italian theatricals." (*Commedia dell'arte*!)

The best summing up of Jung's approach is on the dust cover of Radin's book, which speaks of the trickster myth as an "unashamed and liberating satire of the onerous obligation of social order, religion and ritual."

And what has this to do with Hermes? Contained within the book are 18 pages, an essay by the renowned mythologist Karl Kerenyi entitled "The Trickster in Relation to Greek Mythology." And guess who appears on the scene? Right.

Hermes, says Kerenyi, the trickster among the gods, contains but surpasses all "versions from the lower sphere." The Indian trickster, for example, is a "spirit of disorder, of an enemy of boundaries, a mighty life-spirit. Hermes, too, disregards boundaries, yet he is not a spirit of disorder. And though it would not be wrong to call him a life-spirit it would not be enough."

And now we hear a new voice. It is Kerenyi, but a Kerenyi who in some fashion *knows* Hermes. We've encountered this phenomenon again and again in trying to grasp our god—and of course it is what has befallen us. He starts with the wand, which in the hand of Hermes "has nothing to do with the work of earthly magicians; it is the staff of the psychopomp, of the hoverer-between-worlds."

The trickster hero is picaresque. The trickster god, however, is the source of a "particular way of experiencing the world." This world, "while not contradicting science, yet manages to transcend the scientific view." Things are seen under a special aspect.

The source from which we gain this experience, "whether

we name him or not is Hermes."
Exactly our experience!

SANDY

Let's hear it for Radin, for Jung, for Kerenyi, for Sandy and Rusty and for HIM!

Chapter 4

RUSTY

This is probably a good spot to go into the matter of tricks on our excursions. We both touch upon it here and there in these pages, but we probably haven't made clear its extent and persistence.

Again and again, things go awry at the last possible moment so we don't know whether we can get off or not. Planes are too late to make connection or non-existent or luggage wanders here and there with a mind of its own. Stoppers don't work and hotel engineers can't make them behave. Once we had to change rooms. There must be some esoteric meaning to this, but we've never found it.

Keys don't work or they disappear. As a matter of fact keys always play some part in our adventures. We can't get ourselves into our rooms or our clothes out of our suitcases. Keys of course do have a symbolic significance of importance, but it's the trickster more than the symbolist who busies himself at our expense when it's a question of rooms and suitcases.

Then there are the purses. We decided, early in the game, that we would buy a special small purse in which would be a fifty-fifty amount of cash so we wouldn't have to keep saying, "Your turn." How many purses have we bought—or mislaid or forgotten to pack? We've lost count. This, though not entertaining to us, probably is to Someone. The purse is emblematic, we now discover, of pilgrims, Priapus and Guess Who?

We are in agreement that the most charming (and least distressing) trick has to do with threes. We Three is of course a fact—it exists—but up until now, who knows about it? Nobody. Yet again and again and again, there are three menus on our table, three cups by the coffee machine, three glasses on the sink, three chocolates at bedtime.

But the Santa Fe trip, the trip where we first encountered Radin, was so filled with typical H. tricks that we almost gave up. We had a cottage for a week and although it was supposed to be spring, it was cold. The furnace was welcome, but it wouldn't turn off. Neither would the faucets. There were no blankets or washrags, no forks in the kitchen, a hole in the new kettle. And of course the door wouldn't lock—on the inside. The hotel helpers were stymied and kept saying "This has never happened before." We believed them.

SANDY

On the last day of one of our trips, back East again, we saw pugs.

"So?" I hear you mutter. Well, just you wait, Melanie.

Pugs nowadays are rare. Even one would have stood out, but there were many more than one.

On arriving home Rusty naturally shut herself up at once in her special library. Pugs are "small short-haired dogs with curled tails and wrinkled faces." We all know that, but what followed was unknown to Rusty, to me and, I have no doubt, to you.

A pug is a.) a Puckish character, mischievous and spritely, b.) a slight alert animal such as a hare and c.) someone well loved.

And now hear this:

Puck is often equated with—you can imagine, I'm sure. It was one of those times when Hermes just flashed by—no paper chase, no great revelation, just "I am here."

Oh, Hermes!

RUSTY

Seeing (and contemplating) pugs made me think of dogs in general—not that they are ever far from my mind. For dogs I have profound and unqualified devotion. Just beholding one tends to make my day. Beholding several makes a fiesta.

Some years ago I wrote a paper, "Dog Star," which was read at a Franciscan Service in a tiny lakeside chapel. The chapel was packed with dogs sitting peacefully at the feet or on the laps of their persons. Here is part of what I had to say:

> There is nothing on earth like the dog. From toenail to shoulder the Chihuahua barely achieves six inches while the Irish wolfhound tops the yardstick. The Mexican hairless is naked, the Yorkshire terrier burdened with more than a foot of fur. Legs may be straight or bowed, ears upright or drooping, tails extended like a bell pull or curled like a bedspring, and scales may be tipped at one pound or 150. Moreover, the two hundred known breeds of dog can be found from pole to equator, in city and village, farm, forest and wilderness.
>
> In the halls of academe, this astonishing creature has, of course, a name. It is canis familiaris. A canis is a dog. A familiaris is a friend. A friend, says the dictionary, is "attached to another by feelings of affection." Rarely has the nail been hit so squarely on the head. First encounters between dogs and men seem to have taken place independently, over widely scattered areas of the world and everywhere with the same result. For thousands upon thousands of years, canis familiaris, in all his myriad forms, has been attached to homo sapiens by feelings of affection—surely one of the strangest mysteries of all time.
>
> Piddling and squealing, the puppy staggers straight to his goal, wriggling in ecstasy and lavishing nips and kisses upon any piece of human anatomy he can reach.
>
> The adolescent flings himself upon his idol in a

tangle of paws and a slobber of passion that at best shreds garments, at worst levels the idol with the ground. The adult gazes upon his hero or heroine and repeats the question he first asked before the dawn of history, "How may I serve you?"

He also says, "Whither thou goest, I will go"—given even the slightest encouragement.

Wrote the Apostle Paul to the Corinthians, "Without love I am nothing," and love, he added, "never faileth." We know both statements are true—and we look the other way. We know we should act upon them—and fail to do so.

For the dog there has never been any problem.

"Love is not love," William Shakespeare tells us, "that alters when it alteration finds." And once again we both recognize the truth and admit our inability to go along with it. Not so the dog. Canis familiaris continues to offer love when Dr. Jeckyll turns into Mr. Hyde.

Surely we should be grateful for the dog—this wondrous gift which assures us that love upon this planet—unchanging, undying, unqualified—is possible. Should we not think twice before we persuade him to serve us in ignoble ways? And should we not ponder deeply the ethics of injuring him for some putative benefit to ourselves? What can we force him to do for us that could possibly compare with what he does without force, without persuasion, without even prompting? To misuse so fair a gift so freely given is at the very least graceless.

Too late for my paper, I came upon a striking comment by Ambrose Bierce. A dog, he remarked is "a kind of additional or subsidiary deity designed to catch the overflow and surplus of the world's worship."

Let us not forget that the brightest star in all our firmament is Sirius, the Dog Star.

Shortly after writing this, I discovered we were going on a trip. Hermes had spoken.

Our hotel was on a narrow beach with points of land jutting seaward right and left. On our first morning, round one point came three dogs, unescorted, un-panicked, apparently just enjoying a swim. They re-appeared the next morning. Unescorted dogs began to catch our eyes wherever we went—not wild or gaunt or begging or lost—just going about their business in twos or threes or fours. We had the eerie feeling that we were people in a dog world instead of vice versa. In a little store window were some of the most remarkable dog sculptures we had ever beheld. Dogs are so much a part of our lives that we were startled to perceive them as symbolic. Nevertheless, after all these years we knew a symbol when it appeared.

The dog is companion to the Egyptian god Thoth and Thoth is "identified with the Greek god Hermes." Besides the dog, his chief symbol is the ankh, the key to life, both present and eternal, and to divine wisdom. Thoth is "an instrument of the creator" say the old sources, an awakener and "cleaver of the way." He is also a divine messenger, the inventor of letters and numbers, a regenerator and regulator of time. He is the author of prophetic books and a participant in the ritual of weighing the hearts of the dead.

SANDY

Well, we've thought a lot and learned a lot (and had a gorgeous time doing it), but Hermes, when he decides to make an appearance, always presents something new.

Bermuda. It reminds me of rainbows. I don't know why exactly. Maybe its color—the sea, the sand, green hedges and bright flowers. Or it may be that rainbows are bridges between what we know—or think we know—and what we don't know—or think we don't know.

Anyway, Bermuda was where Hermes made himself known to us. So back we went.

This trip, this paper chase, this revelation was about time. Reservations were made in an enchanting inn on the sea. We took a taxi from the airport almost choked with the usual excitement. On the way we passed a club that had been recommended as a fine place to swim. It was, we noted, about a 15-minute drive from where we were staying (as often happens in Bermuda, a beach that had once enhanced our inn had disappeared in a storm).

We had a cottage, private and inviting, with a balcony over the sea. The fact that the stopper in the bath tub did not function was inconsequential.

The morning was radiant, and, after breakfast on the balcony we took a walk along the beach—and found that the club which had been a 15-minute drive away yesterday was next door. Where had the fifteen minutes gone?

How hard it is to describe such happenings! How could these things be possible when we knew they weren't possible? It is truly unhinging.

That morning Rusty lost her watch on the beach. A

long search was unsuccessful. In the afternoon we went to Hamilton to replace it and there were clocks and watches everywhere. There were diamond watches in shops, alarm clocks on sale, kitchen clocks on walls. There was even a shop that sold framed pictures made of clock parts. I bought an owl and Rusty, a butterfly.

That evening my treasured watch bracelet was gone from my suitcase. I was terribly depressed as it was my "trip" watch and I had worn it on all of our adventures.

The next morning, when we came back from a swim, my watch was on the dresser in our room. Rusty never found hers.

So, Hermes, it is time, isn't it?

Everyone knows that time seems to pass quickly when you are busy and slowly during lonely times, but a 15-minute drive in a taxi to places next door is not the same thing.

But, wait, the last episode was a severe shock.

Rusty had made an appointment for a haircut in town for three o'clock one afternoon. Transportation is a real problem in Bermuda for visitors. Roads are very narrow, so walking or bicycling is dangerous. Taxis are expensive. So, we took a bus to town and arrived at the hairdresser's on time. There was a long discussion about the haircut as Rusty was taking a big step—her hair had always been longish.

Then came the shampoo and set and a considerable time under the dryer. The result was approved, the bill paid, the bus taken back to the other side of the island. When we got back to the inn, we looked at the time and it was 20 minutes past three. The appointment had been at three o'clock.

It was not funny nor even wondrous. It was downright scary, like slipping into another zone. It was not one weird person hallucinating but two people experiencing something totally unreasonable.

We were never, never able to explain this. However, we quite distinctly got the message that time, as we know it, is not to be relied upon.

Of course, time would never mean anything to Hermes in any of its forms. It's a crutch that man invented to give some security and pattern to a bewildering existence. Why would such a concept affect a god?

Also, alas, Hermes has no idea of what the passage of time might mean to two waning mortal females. He still joyfully makes us lose suitcase keys, makes us cope with bathtub stoppers, missed connections and insane situations. It is no longer easy for those of us distant—very distant – from our first youth. But what choice have we?

We did go to the library and looked up "time" in a book of quotations. Herewith:

> T.S. Eliot:
> And indeed there will be time
> To wonder, "Do I dare?" and, "do I dare?"
>
> Horace:
> "Now is the time for drinking—now the time to beat the earth with unfettered foot."

Not too enlightening, but an excellent idea. The morning we left Bermuda we saw a double rainbow.

RUSTY

In the early days of You-and-I long before we met Hermes, we went to San Francisco where myrtle entered our lives as a symbol—and a very striking one.

We found that it has long been revered as a tree of the dead since, being an evergreen, it speaks of life-in-death and therefore of immortality or rebirth. It is the emblem of initiation into Bacchic rites and is particularly sacred to Aphrodite. It is particularly hateful to Hera and Athena because when Paris decided that Aphrodite was the most beauteous of the three, she happened to be all decked out with myrtle leaves.

Through the years we came upon myrtle persistently, but never could see anything to do about it. Then one day out of the blue, Sandy said, "Let's go to Myrtle Beach."

We asked around about it and were told that of all the ruined beaches of the Atlantic coast, it was one of the worst.

So why go? Well, by then we were both immovably determined and, with a reservation at the northern (and less damaged) end, we set forth.

Our room was handsome and the sea was the sea, but the beach in between was entirely covered with scampering, ball throwing, boombox playing, shouting, beer-slugging teenagers and obese, shouting, boom-box playing, beer slugging, sandwich eating middle-agers. It was not inviting.

Our hotel did not serve meals except breakfast, which we only discovered when we were received with hostility in a pleasant dining room open, it rapidly appeared, for an out-of-town bridal party and not for hungry patrons-in-residence. As we strode in, a minister rose to his feet saying, "Now let us pray."

In a search for food we could choose between a five-mile taxi ride and a half-mile walk through a housing development and across an eight lane death trap. We chose the former our first night and the latter our second. It was on the second excursion that we heard the mockingbird. Riveted to the spot we were treated to an exquisite concert, short in length but long in variety. It took the curse off Myrtle Beach—at least for the moment—but it was the following day that rocked us to our souls.

We had decided that two days were really all we could take, so we prepared to set forth for Charleston (always a felicitous You-and-I spot) and settle there for the rest of our trip. Sandy had letters to write, so I went for a final beach walk.

Walking more or less alone (well, as alone as you can get in daylight on Myrtle Beach) I looked over my shoulder for some reason and beheld on the sand a few feet behind me the small, round shadow of a cloud. But there were no clouds in the sky, NOT ONE.

I walked on a bit faster—and abruptly stopped. The shadow was at my heels. I scanned the heavens horizon to horizon. Not a cloud, but the eerie little shadow, round and dark, stayed with me. The experience only ended at the edge of the hotel grounds. Of course we chewed this over and over and then chewed some more. Once in Charleston, we sped to the library and, by way of Aristophanes' play *The Clouds*, we arrived at *The Birds*. No use asking how and certainly not why. This is just the way things work.

And of course it was in *The Birds* that we encountered Cloud Cuckoo Land, the place between heaven and earth where we find ourselves when we are together.

Haven't we always dwelt in a surrealist world, a place where everything is clear, recognizable and perfectly navigable, yet at the same time phantasmagoric? As to birds, haven't they frequently accompanied us, appearing out of nowhere as heart-stopping symbols—eagles, flamingoes, parrots, the mysterious midnight blue bird and now mockers, to say nothing of owls? Yes. But the adventure was not finished.

Strolling the streets of Charleston, we stopped beside a fenced garden, large by Charleston standards and unknown—or at least heretofore unbeheld—by us. There, full-sized and dominating the entire garden, was a statue of Mercury. We stopped beneath a magnolia tree and the music began. A hidden mockingbird sang and sang and sang. A small crowd of strollers gathered as rapt as we were. And when the music finally ceased, all wandered away in silence.

RUSTY (again)

Needless to say, having Hermes in one's life is pretty compelling. Having Hermes in one's life in old age is unhinging. I have to make a constant effort to keep my mind on things to be done.

Sandy faces the same trouble and has three wire baskets on her desk. One says IMPORTANT, one says URGENT and one says RIGHT THIS MINUTE. In one of my mental wanderings I came upon a Hermes memory long forgotten—or at least displaced—since it was pre-Revelation.

Somewhere along my way, I met someone interested in alignments of ancient sites, or "ley lines." Unfortunately, I thereupon talked about this subject so enthusiastically that I ended up agreeing to give a lecture.

This, of course, involved research.

My best source turned out to be a book called *Earth Magic* by Francis Hitching, at the time a member of the Royal Institute of Archeology and the Prehistoric Society.

His book was a stunner not only because he showed us a megalithic society of great range and sophistication, but because he risked his reputation by stating that the leaders of the megalithic world not only understood mathematics and physics but were masters of some mysterious power long lost to us.

What are the meanings of giant standing stones and rocking stones, flawlessly executed mounds, stone chambers, cairns and beacons, and the amazing circular constructions like Stonehenge, hinted at throughout southern Europe and still standing in England? Theories continue to clash as to what they are and even where they are.

Hitching studied the work of a 19th century Englishman named Alfred Watkins, a Justice of the Peace, senior partner in a worthy business, school governor and a Fellow of the Royal Photographic Society. Watkins observed that the extensive remains of the megalithic world in England were aligned one with another. The connecting lines he called leys, and he claimed for the leys a power recognized throughout megalithia. Ley lines, in other words, were the pathway for a form of energy—natural, psychic or a combination of both.

The fact that leys can be located to this day by dowsers put Hitching even further out on a limb from the point-of-view of the scientific world, yet as time goes on there is, here and there, more of a swing toward Hitching than toward the diehard sceptics. The growing verdict is that Mr. Watkins had something.

Hitching, that brave and open-minded scholar, did not stop there. Neither did I. He directed my enthralled (and bemused) attention to a certain John Michell, "one of Britain's best-known proponents of original and unorthodox interpretations of prehistory" and to the work of Sir Norman Lockyer, Fellow of the Royal Society and Director of the Solar Physics Library in Kensington. In the midst of my far-from-simple pursuit, whom did I encounter? Yes.

Hermes, I learned with delight, "the mercurial god of rocks and pillars" was closely associated with standing stones. The Romans found "Mercury stones" set in line over the Etruscan countryside and straight stone-lined tracks leading to "herms" in Greek cities.

Our intrepid ley hunters found close similarities between those of Greece and those of Britain, with Hermes always hovering. With the usual delight one experiences on a Hermes hunt, I presently discovered that once upon a time he was not only known to the Egyptians as Thoth but to the Gauls as Theutotes, "a name still with us in Tot or Toot hills throughout England."

Hermits, insisted one of our fellow diggers and delvers, got their name from their association with Hermes, "acting as guides to pilgrims and travelers." This seems a worthy—or at least helpful—activity, until we discover that the New English Dictionary (whatever that may be) "associates Hermes with the will o' the wisp," the native Puck or hobgoblin who leads travelers down obscure pathways to lose them in bogs and desert places." They were probably crashing bores. All over the world, one of the royal this-and-thats lyrically ends a piece of dense research with, "the ghost of the former mercurial deity looms above the old paths and standing stones."

Wonderful stuff—except for the word *former*. There's nothing former about Hermes. He's now and forever.

SANDY

I have been thinking of *The Dancing Wu Li Masters: An Overview of the New Physics* by Gary Zukav (HarperCollins, 1979). I remember how excited we both got about the book when it first came out. I also remember how much of it I read one spring when Mrs. Musgrove and I were particularly close.

Mrs. Musgrove was a wild pig I brought up after I found her a very small infant, badly injured—probably (as often happens) by a hawk who, having captured her, dropped her for some reason. Though she grew to be very large—and very loving—she was always lame.

On pleasant afternoons, she would sometimes flop enticingly in a shady spot near my house and I would sometimes bring my book, *The Dancing Wu Li Masters* and, using her expansive flank as a pillow, enjoy a good read.

Thinking about all the "impossibles" that we regularly encounter and how hard it is to believe what we know is true, I sought out some notes I had taken:

> If we picture a moving particle, it is very difficult to imagine not being able to measure both its position and momentum. Not to be able to do so defies our common sense. This is not the only quantum mechani-

cal phenomenon which contradicts common sense. Common sense contradictions, in fact, are at the heart of the new physics. They tell us again and again that the world may not be what we think it is. It may be much, much more.

The extraordinary importance of the Copenhagen Interpretation lies in the fact that for the first time, scientists attempting to formulate a consistent physics were forced by their own findings to acknowledge that a complete understanding of reality lies beyond the capabilities of rational thought.

The Copenhagen Interpretation was, in effect, a recognition—a *re*-cognition—of those psychic aspects which long had been ignored in a rationalistic society. After all, physicists are essentially people who wonder at the universe. To stand in awe and wonder is to understand in a very specific way, even if that understanding cannot be described. The subjective experience of wonder is a message to the rational mind that the object of wonder is being perceived and understood in ways other than the rational.

The next time you are awed by something, let the feeling flow freely through you and do not try to "understand" it. You will find that you *do* understand, but in a way that you will not be able to put into words.

Wu Li Masters perceive in both ways, the rational and the irrational, the assertive and the receptive, the masculine and the feminine. They reject neither the one nor the other. They only dance.

Maybe, like the Owl and the Pussycat, "hand in hand on the edge of the strand they danced by the light of the moon."

As did your grandmother and your great-aunt, Melanie, once upon a time.

RUSTY

Have you perhaps wondered, Melanie, whether our research always proved right about the interpretation of symbols? Well, almost but not quite. In dearly beloved Charleston, we once had an experience which, while not wildly colorful in itself, held an almost overwhelming connotation.

I carried my huge You-and-I volumes with me and we read them aloud cover to cover, which we had never done before. Our symbol for this trip appeared right away and was clearly the rabbit. This was extremely odd because we had already met this party years ago and found his symbolism inexplicable. We just tucked him away in our puzzled minds and tried to forget. So why the rabbit all over again?

The light, as always, finally broke. We trudged to the Charleston public library (record temperature at 96 degrees) and with extreme difficulty and the attention of two head librarians, we found the following—Hermes, this time not starting something new but correcting something in the past:

Among trees, we learned the palm, myrtle and apple are sacred to Aphrodite; among plants, the rose and poppy, among birds the sparrow and the swan. As a sea goddess she is attended by dolphins and carries a conch shell (when she isn't carrying a mirror). And guess what! Her land animals are rams or possibly bulls, (slight research confusion here), tortoises and hares!

More than one ancient text mentions the belief that the hare is capable of changing its sex—is, in other words, androgynous.

***

Another curious lesson had to do with forcing a symbol on us over a stretch of time that we were both unwilling and unable to accept. As moon worshippers and early lovers of the unicorn, we greeted sun symbols with at best indifference, at worst hostility. Now with the advent, or rather recognition of, Hermes, we saw these symbols everywhere.

In Key West our eyes were assaulted by eagles—emblematic, we discovered, not only of power and majesty, which was not surprising, but of immortality, which was. The sun entered the story when we read that, to the ancients, the eagle was suspected of being the only creature capable of gazing at the sun and therefore capable of contemplating divine splendor.

If it occurs to you that Key West is not your typical environment for celestial revelations, we hasten to agree. But are any of our meccas?

Cocks were everywhere in evidence, so of course we looked them up. And what did we find? "Sacred to sun gods of practically all cultures." It would be much more genteel to use the word roosters, but not one reference does this.

Lions, most easily recognized as sun symbols, also joined us—in stone, in stores, in galleries and in case all this failed to get the point across, Key West, we discovered, is really hung up on sunsets. Every single evening elaborate and weird events take place. As the sun retires, jugglers and contortionists juggle and contort until darkness overtakes them.

"I can't—or maybe I mean I won't—take this in." I moaned to Sandy.

"But who are we to take up positions on *anything*!" she replied, which of course is true.

One more insight re sun symbolism from one more bit of research: People with blond hair are close to sun deities—hardly surprising to us, since Sandy is a maniacal sun worshipper.

But what about me? Oddly enough, one of our earliest—and most persistent—signs has been red hair, which must apply to me. I finally got around to looking it up and discovered that red hair symbolizes magic. So far so good, but it's a bit troubling to discover that in parts of the world redheads are feared and hated because they are suspected of knowing too much about hidden things.

SANDY

Speaking of research, Melanie, your great-aunt, while ruffling through the pages of a legend or mythology book, sometimes comes upon something she doesn't want to face—something too far-out to cope with.

She'll tell me about it, but then she wants to drop it because, she says, it's TOO MUCH. In struggling to compose this peculiar document, I've several times had to nag her into writing up particularly peculiar oddities. I know how she feels. I also—and often—don't want to explain the inexplicable, but we just have to at least make a stab at it.

"No one will ever believe it," she whines, "and maybe it isn't important." To which of course I have to point out that we don't know what's important.

One of these weird tidbits concerns the Emerald Tablet and she has finally consented to tell about it.

RUSTY

So all right, I was ruffling idly through a dictionary of myths and symbols and suddenly the word emerald leapt out at me. I wasn't looking up anything beginning with an E- and certainly not Em-, but there it was:

"Emerald Tablet: a book on the art of making gold attributed by alchemists to Hermes!"

Well, we already knew Hermes was connected to alchemy, but where on earth and also what on earth was an emerald tablet? We couldn't seem to get any further. I half hoped we could forget the whole thing, but on our very next trip we wandered into a gemstone store and there, staring at us, were two beautiful slabs of something bright green and faintly translucent. We bought them, of course, and again of course, the salesgirl knew nothing about them.

There was a sequel—not right away, but time doesn't matter.

***

A Life of Picasso by John Richardson (Random House, 1991) appeared—a marvel—and although it weighed a ton and cost a mint, I rushed right out and bought it. Volume

One has this to say, referring to a harlequin sketch in which the figure is pointing up with one hand and down with the other:

> Anyone familiar with occult iconography will recognize this upward and downward gesture. It symbolizes the most famous of all mystical axioms, contained in the Tabula Smaragdina (The Emerald Tablet), attributed to the legendary Hermes Trismegistus. Whatever is below is like that which is above, as all things are made from one.

So there we are. Another long, complex paper chase with a stunning re-iteration of the infinite and abiding importance of androgyny.

SANDY

"Why in the world would you want to go to St. Augustine?" a friend asked Rusty. She replied that she had not the vaguest idea but that was where we were going.

"I've never heard of anyone who ever chose St. Augustine for a vacation," the friend persisted. How to explain? She couldn't. We blindly chose a bed and breakfast that described itself in a brochure as a "lovely, interesting old house." An old house it was. Interesting it was.

We arrived in late afternoon and climbed the steps to the front door. The huge door was opened by an ancient woman who informed us that our room was ready but that Peter had gone home. He, she added, would be back in the morning and would carry our bags up the two flights of stairs. Until then we could leave them in the downstairs hall and feel quite free to come down should we need anything.

The ancient lady disappeared.

We decided that it was just as easy to carry our suitcases up the two flights of stairs as to go up and down for our nightgowns and tooth brushes.

The room was spotless and carefully prepared for us—with one exception. On one of the beds was a wrinkled newspaper open to a full page advertisement for an auction of fine bronzes the following Sunday. We dispensed with the newspaper, unpacked and went to bed.

The following morning we rang the desk for room service and got an answering machine with a man's voice. We left, hopefully, a message about breakfast. An hour later the door burst open and in came a girl, extraordinarily charming and, apparently, quite mad. She had trays for us and we were cross and famished.

I told her about the ancient woman and about Peter who wasn't there and the answering machine when we called for breakfast.

"Oh, her!" she giggled and flung herself full length on my bed, upsetting the coffee. "She's the owner. Peter is her son who only comes for an hour or two in the morning. The answering machine is in his house about four miles away."

There was a pause. We waited, breathless.

"What religion are you girls?" she asked. Girls? She pointed to our small bronze statue of Hermes standing on a silk scarf covering the TV.

"He's just a friend," said Rusty.

"Oh" she said. She then sprang up. "I know what would

be just wonderful for you girls. You simply must go to this auction on Sunday." She rustled through a newspaper that she had brought and, lo and behold, there was the advertisement that we had already seen.

She looked doubtfully at a huge statue of a naked archer with a three foot bow. "Maybe they have smaller ones" she said and skipped off.

Saint Augustine is full of Greeks—Athens Street, Hippolyta Street—and Greek restaurants. It seems that Majorcans, in Spanish days, imported masses of Greek indentured servants. In a store attached to the old Greek Orthodox chapel were a thousand Christian books, crosses etc. and one small enchanting box with a head that we knew was Hermes. We took it to a Greek chef and sure enough it was! We also saw three men, young, middle-aged and old, who looked exactly like Hermes. We recognized them at once.

We then fell in love with a fascinating theme found everywhere—an archaic face with long eyes and small, subtle smile surrounded by rays of light. A potter told us (her husband was a history professor) that it was Greek, but very ancient, before Greeks were really what we now call Greek.

(Within a week of her return, Rusty saw in Boston in the Hermes shop an entire window decorated with this theme. Nobody in the store knew anything about it at all.)

Then, quite unavoidably, it was Sunday. There was nothing else to do—we gave in. A cab took us to a huge convention resort where the auction was to be held.

It was vast and deadly. The central building was surrounded by wading pools, exercise rooms, beds of marigolds and a miniature golf course. The building was filled with throngs of people looking alike, examining bulletin boards that told what to do and where to meet.

It was lunch time and we were miles from town and the taxi had left. There was just the one dining room, and it turned out that there was to be a special Sunday jazz brunch. A middle-aged lady clad in shocking pink satin shorts and cobweb tights seated us. She brought us pink champagne in plastic glasses. On the buffet was an array of lunch meats, molded salads, slices of yellow cheese, cottage cheese stained with maraschino cherries.

After an hour, the auction started and went on and on. Everything was oversized—rugs, furniture, unmentionable paintings. Eventually we became tired and terribly bored. It had been a long three hours. No sign of a statue of Hermes or anything that would explain this endless, frustrating day.

At five o'clock, people were still bidding and buying but it really was impossible to stay any longer. We gave up and went out of the auction room door into a small lobby. As always, Hermes is unpredictable.

On a wall directly in front of us was a huge print of the Audubon flamingo. We most certainly had not seen it when we had gone into the auction room. My stiff knees gave way and we collapsed on a sofa underneath the flamingo. And then we saw on a wall at right angles to the sofa a slightly smaller, most beautiful print of one man and two women warriors. It was marked *Hermes Paris* and I think the print maker's name was Abatie. We asked about it at the reception desk, but no one knew anything nor, apparently, had ever noticed it.

The next day we went to a bookstore where we found a copy of Thomas Bulfinch's *Mythology*. We sat down to read about women warriors.

The queen of the Amazons, the greatest of women warriors, was called Hippolyta. Her society was entirely female and I had often wondered how this came about. It seems that all the young Amazon warriors went to the neighbors every once in a while and kept only the girl babies that resulted.

In a store window down the street were some fascinating little figures that lured us inside. One was a woman warrior waving something that looked like our magic wands.

"Who is this?" we asked the clerk.

"Pandora," was the amazing answer.

We returned to Bulfinch and learned the following tale:

> To him and his brother Epimetheus was committed the office of making man, and providing him and all other animals with the faculties necessary for their preservation. Epimetheus undertook to do this, and Prometheus was to overlook his work, when it was done. Epimetheus accordingly proceeded to bestow upon the different animals the various gifts of courage, strength, swiftness, sagacity; wings to one, claws to another, a shelly covering to a third, etc. But when man came to be provided for, who was to be superior to all other animals, Epimetheus had been so prodigal of his resources that he had nothing left to bestow upon him. In his perplexity he resorted to his brother Prometheus, who, with the aid of Minerva (Athena), went up to heaven, and lighted his torch at the chariot of the sun. and brought down fire to man.

With this gift came man's dominion over earth and everything on it. Woman, however, did not yet exist. The story goes that Jupiter (Zeus) dreamed her up to punish Prometheus for stealing fire and mankind for accepting it. Since she was made in heaven, the gods each contributed gifts, Aphrodite proffering beauty, Hermes persuasion, Apollo music, etc. Because of the lavish graciousness of the gods, the woman was called Pandora, which means All Gifted.

Bulfinch:

> Thus equipped, she was conveyed to earth, and presented to Epimetheus, who gladly accepted her, though cautioned by his brother to beware of Jupiter and his gifts. Epimetheus had in his house a jar, in which were kept certain noxious articles for which, in fitting man for his new abode, he had had no occasion.

We know the rest of the story, which of course asserts how dreadful woman has always been in the world of splendid men (remember Eve).

But Rusty has many other books on mythology and when she got home she found something quite different. In Larousse's *Mythology* we learn that Pandora brought the box with her. Moreover, Hermes did not give her the gift of "persuasion" (whatever that might mean) but of "perfidy and lying." She was no namby-pamby girl eaten up with curiosity because she was vain, idle and a trouble-maker, which is the usual meaning of the myth. She was a powerhouse in her own right and we like to think that Hermes was so pissed off about what man could—and would—do with fire that he took a swipe at mankind with a gorgeous woman warrior who knew a thing or two.

RUSTY

As always, I have been chewing away at You-and-I and wondering if we can ever gain attention for so marvelous an experience as ours has been—and is still being.

Sandy has frequently remarked on how afraid of the unknown most people seem to be. Faced with the inexplicable, most members of homo sapiens try to laugh it off, struggle to explain it in dimensional terms, or, in extreme cases, blind themselves to the whole happening.

There is a tale that bears this out.

In the early 16th century, it seems, a huge Spanish galleon appeared off the Mexican coast. The peasants of Tabasco, laboring over their crops, had never seen a ship of any kind (they got about in small rowing boats), never mind an enormous vessel under full sail. Neither had they ever beheld men in armor or horses. The result was that they could not—and did not—see the galleon.

This is well documented, but there are undoubtedly thousands upon thousands of such incidents taking place every hour and everywhere. By and large, homo sapiens cannot see what he cannot at the moment account for. You-and-I are apparently blessed by what—a sixth sense? An inner eye? An open mind that somehow neither discomfort nor ignorance nor even fear can close?

Here, for instance, is my "Behold a Pale Horse" story, which came out in *Yankee Magazine*:

> It was so cold that trees snapped and the house creaked and groaned. A swathe of moonlight lay

across my bed.

I awoke to barking. My bed is a long way from the kitchen where our dogs have always spent the night. The barkers were big, well able to raise a rumpus, yet never before had they woken any member of the family. The clock said 3:00 A.M.

I got up, tied my bathrobe, tried—unsuccessfully—to persuade myself that I could not find my slippers, and started downstairs. There was no need to turn on my lights. Even the corners were lit by blue-white moonlight reflecting off new snow.

I opened the kitchen door. The dogs flattened me against the wall in their fierce rush to the other end of the house.

I followed slowly, my heart thumping. In the living room they were flinging themselves against the glass doors. The curtains were already in shreds. Whatever it was was there.

I grabbed a dog's color and hauled first one and then the other, violently protesting, all the way back to the kitchen. Then I returned to the living room and sat down. Five minutes passed.

I stood, parting the curtains.

Our house is perched on a steep hill. From the living room a flight of brick steps leads down to the lawn. Standing atop the steps, face pressed against the glass, long-lashed eyes looking into mine, was a large horse. He had a well-fed look, sturdy and smooth-coated, and he was almost blindingly white. We stared at each other.

"I can't let you in," I told him. "I just can't let a large horse into the living room. We have a very good rug."

Silence.

"I would put you in the barn, only we haven't got a barn any more. It was collapsing, so we had to tear it down."

Silence. The thermometer read 10 below.

"Look, if you can just hold out for another three hours, I'll start calling. You must belong to someone."

I went back to bed because I couldn't look at him anymore.

At six I started phoning, but I could say only that a horse had been at my house. No large glistening creature now stood atop the steps, and the dogs were quiet. When I let them out, they did not even run around the house to investigate.

I called every farmer and stable owner I knew or whose place I had ever passed or who was listed in the Yellow Pages. I called the U.S. Agricultural Service, the Cheshire County Agricultural Service, the Cheshire County Farmers' Exchange, the U.S. Farm Administration. I called the state police. The Post Office made a note of it. So did the general store.

I was careful to tell about the dogs and the shredded curtains, but I could sense what everyone was thinking.

Late in the afternoon, I took the curtains down and stood holding them for a moment, gazing out at the still, empty scene. And so it was that I noticed something I had not noticed before. There were no hoofprints in the snow. Perhaps the wind had blown snow over them. Perhaps.

SANDY

I have a wonderful example of what Rusty calls trying to explain the strange in plain-Jane or, as she puts it, "dimensional terms." I was in the process of transferring ownership of my island to the state of Georgia. You probably remember how miserable I was, Melanie. I just hated having to do this, but there was no alternative. I would continue living on the island, but I just couldn't be in complete charge any more. After a search of eight years, the state of Georgia seemed the best landlord.

A large sum of money was lacking to close the deal and at the last moment Mr. Robert Woodruff of the Coca Cola company donated it. Now there was no doubt about what I had to do, but I was devastated. Was I absolutely sure I was doing the right thing? I needed one more week to make a final decision.

I went to the beach to take a quiet walk, always my solution to any problem. As I was meandering sightlessly along, I almost fell over a huge, round, heavy, metal disk lying half on the sand and half in the ocean. It was about two feet in diameter, bright red and on it was the familiar legend, COCA COLA. There it was and there was my answer.

I brought the sign back to the house and here to this day it hangs in the hall. It is in perfect condition—not a scratch.

Some months later, a friend brought to visit a man high up in the Coca Cola hierarchy. My friend asked me to tell him the above saga, which I did and took him to see the sign.

"That sign is seventy years old," he said in wonder. "I don't see how it is possible for it to have been where you found it. It's too heavy to float, too shallow to hold air. Why didn't it sink? And, if it did, and was washed ashore, why isn't it scratched? Now let me think—we should measure the underside to see if the amount of air could possibly…"

"Just a minute," I said, unable to resist. "Why do people always have to take something extraordinary and make it ordinary? Human thinking and planning really doesn't have a very good track record and human awareness is proven to be limited. Unknown things are hopeful—it's the known that I dread."

I have not seen him since.

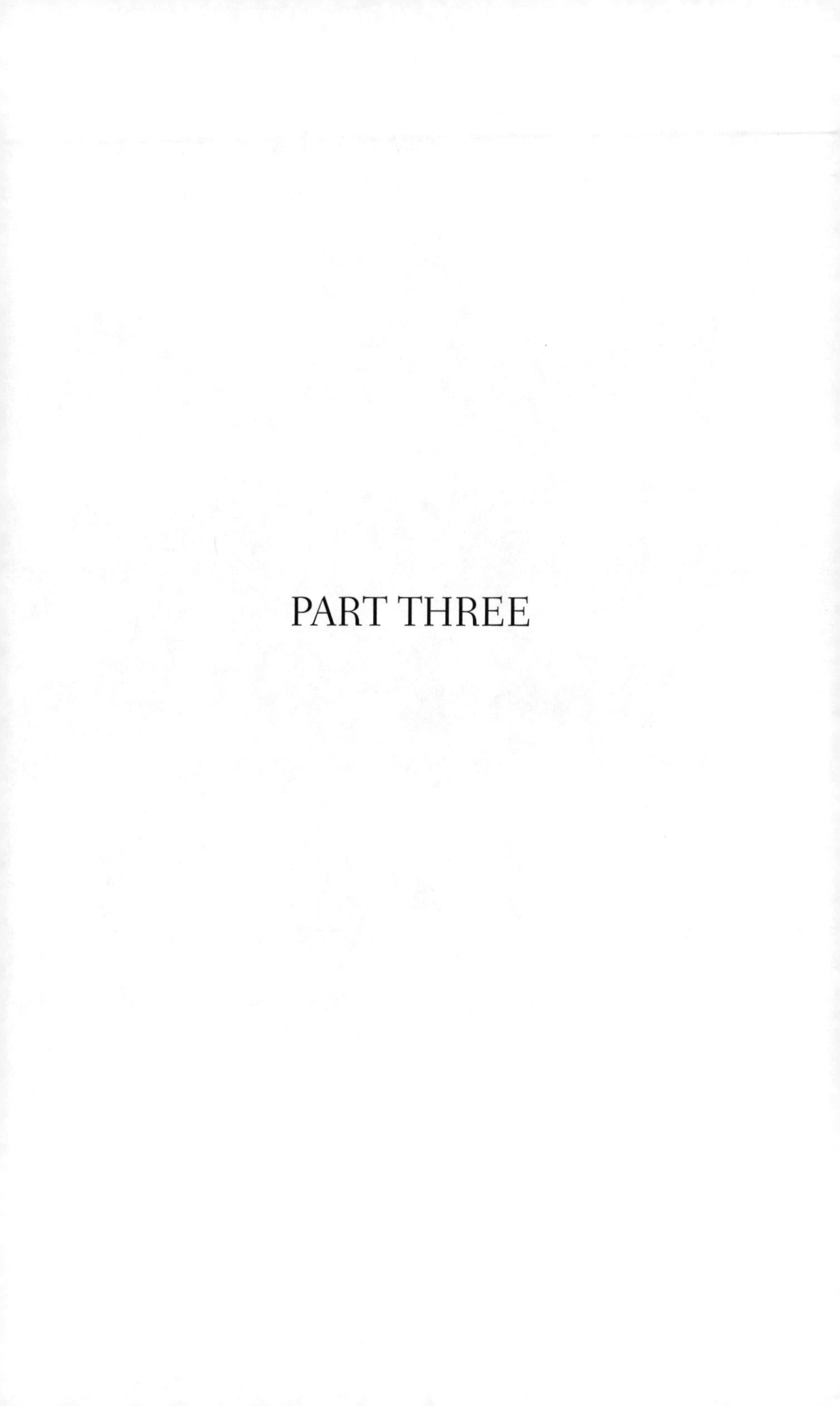

PART THREE

Chapter 1

RUSTY

The great revelation, the "I AM HERMES" revelation was of course an all-time high, but a few years later (quite recently), we received another almost equally stunning.

"Would anyone believe it?" Sandy asked.

"No, but it happened, didn't it?"

"Yes."

So here it is.

We went to Natchez, Miss., where the old houses are gorgeous, where everyone is still fighting the War Between the States and where rich and poor, black and white, old and young, male and female, lose their shirts and much of their sanity on riverboat gambling up and down the Mississippi.

But the You-and-I part was witches. We saw them everywhere—the traditional, narrow-nosed, pointed chin type. But this was clearly just to grab our attention. We went of course to the library, read and read and learned (over and over) that Diana was goddess and inspiration of many witch cults. Diana is the name more than one boy and girlfriend bestowed on me in the growing up years because Betty, my usual nickname, is so obviously unsuitable.

But there's more.

Diana is the Greek Artemis and Artemis is Hermes' sister! Sandy, of course, is his chief love, there can be little doubt that she is an incarnation of Aphrodite. So once again—and I guess for all eternity—we are sisters-in-law.

Deep down I had always thought that things would cool down as we aged. Not at all. Signs and symbols multiply.

For example, along came bears, dear to both of us but particularly to me, whose childhood was dominated by bears and whose library is stuffed with bear books. For the bear, we found, endurance, bravery and strength are the outstanding traits in symbolism, but it's an ambiguous creature and also stands for misanthropy and moroseness.

Among American Indians, the bear stands for immortality. In China, it is a bringer of blessings. By Finno-Ugrics it is called master-of-the-forest, holy hound, honey paw, wise man, fur man. They never call the animal by its name for fear it will become insulted.

Finns call a bear feast a wedding: everyone dresses in festive clothes, but masks are always worn. One does not laugh near a dead bear. Since it is considered not only stronger but more intelligent than man, it is sometimes offered (obviously in cases of great need) to the forest gods. Oaths are sworn by the bear. Our research ended with the discovery that in Greece, the bear is sacred to Artemis.

So, now, we must turn at once to marvelous Arianna's insights into Aphrodite and Artemis—and a few of mine into Hermes.

So.

Artemis (me):

"Artemis is freedom—wild, untrammeled, aloof from all entanglements. She is a huntress, a dancer, the goddess of nature and wildness, a virgin physically and, even more important, a virgin psychologically, inviolable…defined by no relationship, confined by no bond."

It goes without saying that *huntress* is the first word to strike me and is, at first, forcefully rejected and then put aside for future thought. Physical virginity? I've never really grasped why such an enormous fuss has been made throughout history over the hymen. But psychological virginity? Yes, I know full well what is meant both by the two words and those that follow. In this sense I am absolutely Artemis—or perhaps not absolutely because I worry about it. I know I should not be so different from my fellows. I try—sometimes hard, but always, I guess, with limited success. I watch other people, and try to be like them but I'm not other people. Ever. Mea Culpa.

"Apollo and his twin sister Artemis are the eternal adolescents. The longing for freedom is the essential Artemisian urge; the longing for clarity, the essential Apollonian passion. They are both distant gods, detached and aloof, at a loss in the world of commitment."

Well, I don't know. Neither a longing for freedom nor a passion for clarity seems adolescent to me. Or perhaps I react negatively because adolescent has become a pejorative—stubborn, rude, cruel, rebellious-without-a-cause. Arianna, it comes to me, probably uses the word just to denote a period. If she does, then I'm with her. From 13 to 18 I mightily longed for freedom and would certainly have shared with a twin, or anyone else, the passion for clarity. I still long for Artemisian freedom and Apollonian clarity, but now know these are goals only gods can reach.

"She is much more at home with animals than with people," I read, "and uneasy in our everyday world."

Unqualifiedly true.

She is a daughter of Zeus, which would, I should imagine, provide her with both power and self-sufficiency. According to Arianna Stassinopoulos, however, these qualities were established by the circumstances of her birth. Born first, with no problems, and, barely a few moments old, she becomes her mother's midwife, "assisting over nine agonizing days and nights at the birth of her brother."

Because of this, Artemis has become the protectress of women in childbirth. Now this I find fascinating. My deep sympathy with what women have to go through, bearing, producing and caring for infants is one of the reasons I have, all my life, felt fury at the predicament of the world's poor, resolutely denied (mostly by males but also by blinkered females for theological reasons) access to contraception.

Part of Artemis certainly never grew up. For playmates, her father gave her the 60 daughters of a benign weather deity. (Not, please, an Olympian deity. It's important to remember these were limited in number.) Part of Rusty never grew up, that's for sure. I love to teach children happy things like acting and dancing and I continue to find delight in my doll houses, known to a puzzled but affectionate acquaintance as my "alternate lifestyle."

Incidentally, the maidens who served as playmates were known as little bears. This persistent bearhood of Artemis strikes a familiar note. Bears are precious to me as well as to her and if I were truly a goddess I too would certainly choose bears as one of my identifying symbols. After very many decades, I still bitterly resent my mother for disposing of my two huge bears without consent because I was "too old."

"There is passion behind Artemis' remoteness, but it is a passion directed not at relationships but at the search for one's self, one's soul in solitude and separateness."

Artemis, Stassinopoulos goes on, "is the goddess of distance, of inviolable boundaries. She embodies the wildness both of nature and of human nature. It is a wildness that conceals great riches but its savagery cannot be evaded."

I know all this, word for word, but also know how to put on the brakes—in fact, they're on all the time. I suppose everyone else's are too, so my dark side is not as dark as Artemis'. She, who is after all an Olympian, has no need of restraint and so whenever she chooses can show "no empathy, no allowance for motive and intention, no hesitation or second thoughts."

But oh, the "exhilarating sense of freedom—freedom from the mass of commonplace opinion, freedom from what binds us to the past, freedom from what is conventionally expected of us in the future."

Arianna knows that for most people there is "fear in this radical confrontation with ourselves, not only fear of loneliness but also fear of what we may discover in these unexplored regions, and we long to escape…But the solitary call of the soul cannot be stifled; only through it can we find the freedom that Artemis in her highest form embodies."

Yes.

But what about the hunting? What can it possibly mean—especially for one who is both patroness and protectress of all nature? Clearly Stassinopoulos is troubled, too, and quotes Karl Kerenyi in *Facing the Gods*.

Referring to Artemis' companions he says, "In the figure of the great huntress the little human bears met a new aspect of their feminine nature. It was a meeting with something wild and vigorous…" Or is it a metaphor for the ceaseless seeking that compels us Artemisians?

Well, maybe, but for me the mystery remains. Only Artemis—or her brothers Hermes and Apollo—can enlighten if they so desire, which they probably don't. Maybe I'm supposed to work it out for myself.

Before closing, one more tidbit. Sacred to Artemis (and also to Apollo) is the quail—rather a long trip from bears. Oddly enough, this tiny creature is a symbol of resurrection.

Time for the endlessly recurring dialogue which I can now carry on without my cohort in the flesh.

"Is this really happening?"

"Yes."

"Am I really an incarnation of Artemis?"

"It's pretty striking, isn't it? You're at least a semi-incarnation, that's for sure."

"But I knew nothing—nothing at all about Artemis."

"That's what makes it real, isn't it?"

"Well, here we go, then. Let's hear it for Aphrodite."

"Cor!"

But you know what? I'm going to give Apollo an innings

first. Why? Because he's my twin brother and I know almost nothing about him. Then there's the matter of the sun symbol that we have puzzled over and even (who do we think we are?) attempted to reject.

First of all, I am beginning to perceive with the kind of insight that probably overtakes anyone attempting to deal with symbols, deities and Greek thought. Artemis is a moon goddess and Apollo a sun god, so they are of course twins "expressing the essential idea that all pairs of opposites are integrated with Oneness." Androgyny—that wise, brilliant, infinitely sophisticated concept!

Just to show my independence, I studied Apollo in Larousse's ten-pound *Encyclopedia of Mythology*—very rough going because Monsieur Larousse hates committing himself and so gives us this version and that version and the little one over there. But here is what I gleaned:

Apollo is always beardless, golden-haired and exceedingly beautiful as to both face and form. Like Artemis, he flaunts bows and arrows and uses them regularly, more on humans than on animals. But, like the sun itself, he is more beneficent than malevolent. Cirlot says didactically that the sun is potentially good and the moon potentially evil, but I'm not going to feel guilty because I don't think any woman would say any such thing.

Apollo is never alone. His retinue consists of the nine Muses and he is not only blessed by their exalted company but partakes of their talents—history, poetry, music, astronomy, eloquence, acting, writing, comedy and tragedy. He is also able, when he so desires, to prophesy (and is apparently jealous of anyone else's skills along such lines). Certain animals are in his charge, but they are herd, not wild, beasties.

His love affairs take up a lot of space but may not have taken a lot of time because they never seem to have amounted to much—no world-well-lost and certainly no ecstasy. He is, was and obviously ever will be a very civilized god.

And here suddenly I come upon something pretty exciting (and, exhausted as you may be by this time, Melanie, you'd better be able to go on reacting with fervor because there's plenty more scintillating stuff to come). Since Stassinopoulos can bring the god to life better than anyone else, I return to her for an Apollonian wind-up and discover this:

"It is irrational not to recognize the irrational, and dangerous…as well. When the Apollonian *know* thyself is united with the Dionysian *be* thyself, when reason is reintegrated with our stubbornly neglected spirit and intuition, then we will have achieved the wholeness in which lies healing and renewal. It was a wholeness achieved at Delphi through the union of the two gods." And under a lovely photograph of Delphi are the words, "Despite the sharp opposition between their two realms, Apollo the god of reason and Dionysos the god of ecstasy were joined together at Delphi."

So now I must make the acquaintance of this new party.

His birth was somewhat unusual because his mother was just a human person and died from the attentions of Zeus (yes, still another brother). The fetus in her womb was removed by its father and placed within his thigh until ready to be born. Was this weird tale, like the birth of Athena, (greatest of the goddesses) from Zeus' head a way of saying, "See, the king of the gods was androgynous too?" I think so. All things contain their opposites. What a relief to step (or be pushed) into the world of Oneness after spending a lifetime wandering in the dark schisms of monotheism!

Anyway, he was born, grew up and entered the world of Olympos—the last god to do so. He may or may not have been welcomed there, for he was looked upon—and still is looked upon—with deep suspicion. He stands for that which is wild in us and that we attempt to stifle, branding it uncivilized.

"The Dionysian revolt began in the 19th century with Nietzsche's *Birth of Tragedy*," writes Stassinopoulos (yes, I'm back with *The Gods of Greece*—impossible to stay away). "And Jung established the 'Dionysian' as a basic structure of our psyche…However hard we oppose, suppress or resist him, Dionysos is invincible."

This god who "destroys those who try to hold him in bondage is also the benevolent god who rewards with life and abundance those who recognize his divinity and his power."

"Dionysos is the god of ecstasy, dance and song…He brings plasticity and flexibility into what is rigid and hard…And the infinite vitality that had been locked away wells up from the depths like the milk, honey and wine that spurt from the earth."

The wine of course is the problem.

"The double nature of the god was symbolized by the double nature of wine." This hardly needs explication, and neither the Greeks nor the patron of the nearest liquor store would quarrel with the statement that "the bringer of liberation, ecstasy, inspiration and the most blessed deliverance is also the bringer of madness."

But Dionysian liberation is not dependent on booze. He can free and inspire without resorting to the grape. He dances, he sings, he shouts with glee and he can thrust us "into a new life, overflowing with rapture and vitality," always providing we will risk what we "cling to for security."

I see us prancing down streets in the early days of You-and-I (all right, and only yesterday as well), enraptured just to *be* and of course it was Dionysos. And Apollo was there too—wine and libraries, laughing so hard we couldn't bestir ourselves to get on with things and then talking, talking, talking—orienting ourselves in the universe.

And here is something unexpected and cheering:

In ancient Greece it was "the women whose lives were most confined" who became the most enthusiastic Dionysians. He lured them from their looms and again and again "we come across Argive women, Rhodian women, Athenian women ripped loose from the humdrum, orderly activities of their domestic lives and, intoxicated by the god, being transformed into enraptured, manic dancers in the wilderness of the mountains."

Well, good for them—and good for him!

But what is so marvelous, so right about the Greek gods is their individuality, the impossibility of second-guessing them. Dionysos believes in love with all his heart—so much so that he is sometimes called the god of women. Alone among the gods, he remained faithful to his beloved, the Cretan princess, Adriadne, whom he married and immortalized. He was not, you see, acting out anything so gross as getting drunk and screwing around.

And now, finally, to Delphi. Stassinopoulos:

> Antagonism among the different gods runs through the whole of Greek mythology, and the clas-

> sic conflict that has dominated Western literature and has even entered our everyday language is the conflict between Apollo and Dionysos...between the need for order, balance and clarity and the instinct for freedom, ecstasy and exaltation. The vivid lesson of the Greek myths and of Greek tragedy is that unless both gods are given their due, there is a high price to pay. The need for their reconciliation was even institutionalized in Delphi. Delphi was Apollo's home but, during the winter months, he ceded his shrine to Dionysos...the need for Dionysian ecstasy was given its sanctioned place in Apollonian order so that it would not rise out of its neglected depths and overthrow it.

On the pediment of Apollo's temple, he is depicted on one side with his mother, his sister Artemis and the Muses. Opposite is Dionysos and his Maenads.

Would I have come upon all this by myself? Well, yes, I suppose I might have, but would I have taken it in? Not in a thousand years. Hermes has not only showed himself to us and showed us who, in his world, we are, but also introduced us to his brothers.

Usual litany: "Do I believe all this?"

Usual answer: "How can I not?"

Chapter 2

RUSTY (still carrying on):

Aphrodite. Truly. At last.

Larousse says, that the oldest, the Homeric, tradition claimed that she was another child of Zeus but "popular imagination could scarcely be satisfied with so poor a legend and the Homeric tradition was thus supplanted by another, richer in popular appeal."

Richer, maybe, but pretty horrendous because the final myth established her birth from severed genitals flung into the sea. Whose genitals—and why—is too complicated to go into right now, and in any case doesn't matter. For the Greeks, Aphrodite and genitals go together. I am a bit undone by the statement that being born of Zeus was a poor show. On the other hand, it's easier to handle than

Aphrodite's startling arrival.

When the gods first beheld this newest member of the clan, they were overcome; this was natural because "Aphrodite exuded an aura of seduction," writes a lyrical Larousse.

And so does Sandy—or did, anyway (though it's still lurking somewhere when she chooses to call upon it).

Aphrodite, Larousse continues, "stirred all the gods, but it was Hephaestus, the ugliest and most graceless among them, who obtained her for a wife." This came about as a result of a complicated bit of blackmail which, in the end, did Hephaestus little good.

"He is," says Stassinopoulos (who customarily deals in the present tense), "the only Olympian who works. The other gods…make things happen, but they do not work in the consuming sense that our modern era understands the word."

"Hephaestus is the embodiment of man's unquenched creativity—the creativity that forged the bridge between our primordial dependence on nature and our industrial world. He is the symbol of endless resourcefulness and prodigious productivity."

He cannot, however, attain Aphrodite's affection or even perform properly in her bed—or, it seems, anyone else's. Stassinopoulos here makes an arresting comment:

> Modern man is living out both sides of the Hephaestus archetype. He has created the supreme technological civilization and, at the same time, he has spawned a whole industry of sexual manuals, sexual aids and psycho-therapeutic tools. He has created artificial intelligence on earth and has sent man to the

> moon, but he can hardly make love without the help of Masters and Johnson, or maintain a loving relationship without recourse to the technologists of intimacy.

And our neighbors and fellow countrymen think the gods are dead! Not the Greek gods, no sirree.

Back to Aphrodite. Excuse absence.

Marriage did not hinder her affairs, though, oddly enough, she was one of the deities who presided over the sanctity of marriage. Neither Larousse nor, so far as I can discern, the Greeks explain this oddity. "She took a wicked delight," Larousse tells us, "in rousing the passionate desires of the immortals and launching them on amorous adventures."

Hermes is her most famous lover, but there were others. Even females were occasionally launched, though all my sources agree that not only Athena and Hera but also Artemis and Hestia (goddess of home and hearth) did not, after an evening with Aphrodite, automatically set forth looking for trouble. Earthly lovers were of course legion.

Stassinopoulos, (impossible to stay away), writes that the heavenly Aphrodite/Venus arising from the sea has inspired hundreds of poets and artists through the ages, but it is the earthly goddess who,

> ...through rapture, magic and desire, has held sway over men's lives. Aphrodite embodies sexuality free of ambivalence, anxieties and self-consciousness, a sexuality so natural and quintessential to her that no myth deals with her virginity or its loss...She is the goddess of all arts that enhance beauty and love-making—of perfume and incense, love-charms and potions, the use

> of oils and cosmetics and all the lore of aphrodisiac drinks and foods.

And adds Larousse, the three Graces were not only part of her retinue but she could "make use of their services when she wished to adorn herself in all her seductions."

Unless Sandy is very carefully keeping something from me, I have not yet seen her involved with either celestial helpers or aphrodisiac food and drink, but at the word potions, I saw Queenie as clear as day.

Aphrodite, say the myths, was exceedingly irritated by those foolish enough to believe themselves immune to romance. For example "she caused the women of Lemnos, who neglected her, to exude a foul odor." On the other hand, the goddess herself "is not immune from the wounds she inflicts and the passions she inspires. She is the longing she causes as well as the cause of longing."

Her love for Adonis, the beautiful youth who perished,

> ...has inspired some of the most moving and sensual poetry in Western literature...Loss and death, unrequited love and abandonment, are all part of Aphrodite's realm...Permanence is of Hera's world, not Aphrodite's. What belongs to her is a deep acceptance that passionate love does not last forever, and an equally deep acceptance that man is made to love.
>
> Aphrodite's essence is transformation through the power of love. (It) is the same power that brings destruction, the almighty desire that forgets the whole world for the sake of the beloved... .It is the divine madness that removes the vagueness and dullness of habitual perceptions...In the same way that all matter

> at a certain degree of heat becomes luminous, all men have experienced moments in their lives when they have felt the power of Aphrodite.

So there we are—or rather there Sandy is.

At this point, I know that she is less satisfied than I am—or maybe I should say less persuaded? Less at home in the part? Although she accepted my recognition of her as an incarnation of the goddess Aphrodite, she has never entirely settled in. But that's without doubt just why she is the prototype of the enchantress and wields such power. If she saw herself as others see her, she would probably be intolerable.

Oh, two more bits and pieces. Well, not really bits. They're pretty large:

1.) Aphrodite, along with Hera and Athena, was heavily involved with the Trojan War—probably the most famous contest of all time. This was not very constructive of them (though their presence gave birth to marvelous poetry and drama), but it is worth noting that their participation at no time had anything to do with theology.

While we're at it, another less than praiseworthy activity indulged in by Aphrodite was a pretty torrid series of interludes with the gorgeously handsome Ares, god of war. Everyone, of course—gods and homo sapiens alike—had to pretend to hate him, but Aphrodite, the least hypocritical of beings, enjoyed the affair immensely.

2.) It grieves me to have to tell you that a number of sources suggest that Aphrodite, (never Artemis), was once the Great Goddess, the greatest of the great—the Earth Goddess.

She lost this role, of course, when the patriarchal divinities took over. So, all right. We know who we are, but this is purely evasive. Who, Heaven (or rather Olympus) help us, is Hermes?

Two words pop into my mind. One is construction and the other is discovery. I am captured, profoundly intrigued in that special way that we know so well. I ponder and here we go.

There is a very great difference between discovery and construction. We discover something already there—land, a mathematical fact, color, death, jungle creatures, musical sounds, fire, diamonds, talents, sex. Constructions are man-made, though they are always built from pieces which, being discoveries, are already there. Philosophies, theologies and machines are constructions, though the ideas—and physical laws—on which they depend are discoveries. Constructions can be creative or destructive, of infinite value or utterly useless, or they may play all these roles at different times. Discoveries simply are. They can be appreciated or rejected, loved or hated, but not changed. Constructions can be altered by human thought or hand.

It seems to me that it would be valuable to understand this, particularly when contemplating the gods, including God, the monotheists' deity always spelt with a capital.

Let's anyway try it on for size.

What the monotheists have discovered is a cosmos so clearly obedient to certain laws that a common source seems obvious. Modern scientists agree—up to a point. The Beginning-of-it-all they call the Big Bang, an initial explosion responsible for the whole wild, whizzing, whirling universe, but they make no slightest effort to explain the bang. Scientists do not deal with the word why when contemplating beginnings. This is where construction comes in. Monotheists call the Big Bang the Unmoved Mover, an all powerful entity who is not only responsible for the whole shebang, but planned it expressly for one species on a single planet. The entity, moreover, (called God), can not only be contacted by the species at any time, but, according to Christians, once appeared among them as one of their own.

Polytheists of all persuasions (and there have always been many more of them than of monotheists) wrestle with the problem of Beginnings, but do not buy the concept of a single entity as true in the way that two apples plus two apples make four apples. Like scientists they feel unable to explain the heart of the matter, but unlike scientists they can't leave it alone. They solve their dilemmas with myths and metaphors, marvelous poetic efforts that say, "This aspect of things looks like this, or feels like that or sounds like what's going on over there."

The Greeks discovered the existence of forces that influence homo sapiens. They constructed personalities to clothe the forces and stories to make them recognizable. It is hard to measure the exact proportion of discovery to construction in the make-up of the Olympian gods, but whatever it is, the formula seems the same for them all.

Zeus is Head Honcho. Though powerful, he is not All-Powerful, being frequently frustrated by events and fellow deities. Hera is marriage, stability, the community (though she had a very rough time coping with her husband's law-unto-itself machismo).

Hephaestus is work. Hestia is hearth and home. Apollo is physical beauty, mental clarity and spiritual harmony. He is, in other words, the male ideal—at least to the Greeks.

Athene is wisdom, stand-on-your-own-feet strength. She represents civilization at its best—what it might be but seldom is. She is beautiful as well as wise, the female ideal—which is fascinating because it's the modern feminist ideal, but for our particular Greeks an ideal only manifest in their arts of drama and sculpture—never in real life.

Poseidon represents what is ancient and primitive in us, the ever present bottom line. Water, (rightly) is always seen as the source.

Demeter is motherhood.

Ares is aggression.

Artemis is freedom.

Aphrodite is love.

Dionysos is madness, ecstasy, subterranean forces in us that we suppress at our peril.

Hades is god of death, the only certainty our lives hold and therefore perhaps the most noteworthy (though certainly the least popular) of the gods.

Who, then, is Hermes?

SANDY and RUSTY

We really struggled with this one: Well all right, who *is* Hermes?

"He represents what doesn't fit," we agreed when we first faced this question fair and square. "He's the only god without a specific area." This is pretty perceptive if we do say so. It's also a good place to start.

We've read a lot about him by now and what we surmise seems to hit the nail. It also makes any who-is-Hermes-what-is-he effort pretty tricky. Here are the perceptions of those scholars and tellers of tales (ancient and modern) who have crossed our paths—or rather whose paths we have crossed. Incidentally, there is general agreement that he figures in more stories than any other god.

He's first and foremost the Great Connector. There's general agreement about this too. As Chief Messenger of the gods, he connects heaven and earth, words which are of course metaphors for the seen and the unseen, us and them. As psychopomp, he connects life with death, joining opposites, the heart and essence of androgyny.

Alchemists always saw Hermes as their patron. To connect, when you think of it, is to transform or, in the case of alchemy, to transmute, isn't it? Things are never what they seem at first glance or at first experience or at first thought. Think of the countless times and countless ways this message has been given to us!

He is always moving. There are wings on his feet and wings on his head to tell us so. Yet he is also symbolized by stones. Herms, stone columns with his head on top, were placed all along Greek highways, particularly at crossroads because that is where we move from one realm to another. It was accepted practice to leave a stone near the herm in his honor. The Greeks had some long lost insight into this strange business (long lost to us anyway), that connected stone and motion, but not until modern science got the show on the road could interested people like us grasp it.

Matter, we are now told (constantly), is condensed energy. Energy and mass, like particles and waves, are not enemies but two aspects of one reality. Hermes is indeed the Great Connector—not just of this-and-that but of what seems to us eternal opposites, mankind with the denizens of Olympos, our world with the nether world, matter with energy, most awesome of all, life with death. Of all the gods, he is the most gifted, the most adroit, the brightest and cleverest, yet he serves his fellow deities.

He is all powerful, yet he doesn't depend on power to accomplish his ends—another juggling with opposites, or maybe here we're dealing with paradox. We looked it up to be sure this was the word we wanted and it is. Paradox: a proposition seemingly self contradictory but in reality expressing truth.

And still more thoughts reagarding connection. Though male, he has profound rapport with the way women both experience life and try to live it—not, in other words, the flat statement, the fist on the table, the trampling foot, but rather the subtle path.

To the Greeks, Hermes was both old and young. Statues of the god are barely out of adolescence, while the heads set on roadside herms are bearded and look old—but wait! The tall, stone, columnar herm, we learn, is a gigantic erection! Life, of course, always and inevitably contains both youth and age, birth and death, creation and decomposition.

"The king is dead! Long live the king!" a friend suggested recently. "Is your god perhaps the god of life?"

Is he? It feels that way, though we hardly know how to reach out and touch such a conclusion.

But once again, Hermes eludes any final wrapping up. Everything we've read points to him as the god of the unexpected. At this point, the word serendipity popped up. Knowing only vaguely what it means, we hauled out the dictionary.

Serendipity: the finding of valuable and agreeable things not sought—a word coined by Horace Walpole in a tale called *The Three Princes of Serendip*. The princes in their travels were always discovering by chance things they did not seek.

Would it be possible to find a more right-on description of our acquaintance with Hermes?

Gooseflesh.

What is he like? That's pretty difficult to get down on paper, but if you've been hard pressed by him for most of your adult life, you're willing to give it a try.

The theme of unexpectedness seems to run through just about everything we know about him. Sometimes he is seen as the god of becoming. Hermes' world is one of flux, of who-knows-what's next, of demolishing old ideas and customs to make room for the new. The true Hermes lover and follower (us, for instance) is alert at all times lest something of value be missed. Treasures may be stumbled over, so watch where you put your foot. And whatever you find, never rest content. Under the treasure, or near it heavily disguised, may lie a clue or a vision of incalculable value. To the Greeks, everything was a miracle, the extraordinariness of the ordinary is maybe the best way to put it. But you have to be in a state of openness to recognize the hidden.

Everything about Hermes is unexpected. In ancient Greece, any sudden windfall was a hermaion, the gift of Hermes. As a major god (maybe *the* major god, and maybe there's no maybe about it) he should at all times be awe-inspiring.

Instead, he is a trickster. Hermes loves tricks—the unsuitable, the mischievous. It is hardly surprising that Pan is his son. He can be elegant, magnificent, majestic. He can also be capricious, maddening, playful as a child. In fact, there seems to be a general feeling among Hermes watchers that if you lose all your childishness you lose all chance of even glimpsing his footprint.

Hermes, it seems, can be a liar and a thief. All Hermes admirers are agreed about that. While still an infant, remember, he crept from his cradle in the darkness, stole and hid his brother Apollo's herd, flatly denying any knowledge of the deed. This babyhood adventure is a clear forerunner of the adult Hermes' lying and thieving activities—designed to shake up the serene, the haughty and the settled among his acquaintances.

He is known far and wide as "the god of mystic knowledge" and there is constant reference in antiquity to "hermetic writings," which are ancient metaphysical works dealing essentially with the idea of the close community of all beings and objects.

Finally, he is a seducer. He adores the female but never, under any circumstances remains in bondage to either sex. So great is his charm that he is the only son of Zeus' extensive brood of bastards that Hera not only tolerates but loves.

Ciao!

PART FOUR

Chapter 1

RUSTY

It is time to stop. We're both agreed about that. We're too ancient to keep on postponing the Final Version. But once again…

Out of the blue John Horgan's *The End of Science* was thrust upon me. It is a superb book, an everyone-must-read book. It is full of quotes, but one in particular rocked us.

Do you recall, dear Melanie, very early in this opus, the tale of our pendants: first of our symbols and then how we decided to inscribe them with *Ne Plus Ultra* without the *Ne*, which we interpreted as "This Far and Further?"

Well, here's what Horgan has to say:

"Francis Bacon, one of the founders of modern science, expressed his belief in the vast potential of science with the Latin term *plus ultra,* 'more beyond.' " But *plus ultra*, Horgan believes, is not constrained to science. "It applies, rather, to our imaginations. Although our imaginations are constrained by our evolutionary history, they will always be capable of venturing beyond what we know."

SANDY

And then along came angels.

A friend sent me a book by Theodora Ward called *Men and Angels* (McIntosh and Otis, Inc., 1969) just when Rusty was sent *Angels: An Endangered Species* by Malcolm Godwin (Simon and Schuster, 1990). Most people would undoubtedly make much of so odd a coincidence, but by now for us this kind of thing is just all-in-the-day's-work. I sat right down and sent Rusty a quote, and of course she did likewise. Here is what I sent, quoting Ward:

> The seventh century biographer Muirchu assumed that the angel Victoricus was with Patrick from the beginning of his religious life during his serfdom. He even claimed that the angel visited him 'on every seventh day of the week; and as one man talks with another, so Patrick enjoyed the angel's conversation.' This may not be far from the truth, for some who are sensitive to the movements within their own inner depths find there a seemingly separate personality to whom they can turn for wisdom greater than their consciousness is capable of. In the book *Experiment in Depth*, P.W. Martin describes this helpful figure as

> experienced by certain persons in all cultures, from that of the Greeks of the classical period to that of the American Indians.

The figure has many names, Martin writes. It is Hermes, "the *psychopompus*, the conductor of souls, as Virgil conducted Dante in the infernal regions; it is the daimon on which Socrates placed his trust, the figure of the genius to the Romans, the 'angel of the Lord' of the Hebrew Scriptures, the guardian angel of Christian belief."

And here is what Rusty sent, quoting Godwin. It is certainly not what one would expect in a book about angels:

> One might say that faith is created by fact, or that by observing a phenomenon scientifically an observer can build up an idea of how it works and what it is. But modern scientists are discovering that the world is not quite so simple and that often fact is created by faith. Quantum physicists know that if they expect a particle to act like a wave, it does. If they expect it to act like a point, it likewise accommodates their idea. This is partially due to the fact that any method of observing the world necessarily changes our perception of it. More fundamental is the notion that we cannot step outside of the universe to observe it. We are part of our own experiment.

And then:

> Angels are…indivisible from their witnesses. The Swedish mystic Swedenburg once said: "I am well aware that many will say that no-one can possibly

> speak with spirits and angels so long as he is living in the body; many say it is all fancy, others that I recount such things to win credence, while others will make other kinds of objection. But I am deterred by none of these: for I have seen, I have heard, I have felt."

Rusty then remarks (in case I didn't know, which of course I didn't) that seraphs are the highest order of angels and, according to Godwin, "vibrate at the highest angelic frequency…"

The image of this angelic order, Mr. Godwin continues, is the serpent, who

> …symbolizes rejuvenation through its ability to shed its skin and reappear in a brilliant and youthful form…Two snakes curl around the legendary caduceus…which originally appeared as a wand in the hand of the universal Indo-European God Hermes…The Greek Hermes was the self-same deity as the Egyptian Thoth, the Roman Mercury and the later Archangel Michael who was also a seraph.

And Rusty ends up with some final words quoted gleefully from Godwin, since they refer to two passions of hers: Ley Lines and Canines, oddly linked:

> Many of the shrines dedicated to Mercury/Hermes were sited on top of hills. On their ruins were built the chapels and churches dedicated to Michael…The many "Michael's Mounts" to be found throughout Europe and Britain attest to the power of that ancient archetype, the mound of the dead. Many of the sites

> were, in more ancient times, the focal points of Earth Forces.

And then, without introduction or explanation, no before and no after, comes this:

"Hermes ascended to Heaven in the form of Sirius, the Dog Star."

Chapter 2

RUSTY

I said in the very beginning of this effort, Melanie, that we felt it was important to get it all down while there was still time, but there's more at stake than just getting it down.

The adventure means something, so once again let me say we can discern footprints if we look down, pathways if we look ahead, starlight, moonlight and odd shaped rainbows if we look up. We haven't become missionaries and we certainly aren't busy developing any kind of doctrine. We have, however, been brought to see a lot of stuff we don't think, stuff that gets in the way of shimmering truths almost lost but still lurking.

Enemy Number One—or what seems Number One

to us—is modern science, beginning with physics and chemistry.

The pursuit of scientific facts has taken over our society. Money cascades forth from the government purse, never mind the purpose (if any) of the undertaking. If it comes under the heading of science we've got to underwrite it, no matter how far out, extravagant or dangerous to the welfare of Earth.

Our institutions of learning can raise millions—even billions—for new buildings equipped with state-of-the-art laboratories and machinery, and of course, new faculty. Physics and chemistry are rammed down the throats of budding flutists, poets, foresters, philosophers, historians and weavers.

Libraries are enlarged not because there aren't enough shelves for music scores and poetry or treatises on trees or on life and death or on history or looms, but because there isn't enough for physics, chemistry and all the -ologies old and new. And since advanced science and advanced mathematics are wedded, the budding historian is halted in her tracks by dizzying equations which bewilder her and for which she has no use. Aren't addition and subtraction, multiplication and division enough for the vast majority of us? Of course they are.

The old goals of science were to discover how things work and to discern—or perhaps *interpret* is a better word—the workings of the cosmos. To be just, I should say that there are still such men and women, but they are the minority. The majority appears to be hell bent on the exploitation of scientific findings leading on to the CONQUEST OF NATURE, as if any of us could survive such an outcome. When we have wrung Earth dry, we'll be presumably ready to sail off into outermost space and get to work on the rest of the universe, "we" by that time being cloned or genetically altered robots like the characters in Huxley's *Brave New World.*

Let's face it: Mankind's present approach to science is close to addiction, or one might go further and say idolatry.

And what do these idols teach us? Size, speed and struggle.

The universe is billions of years old and contains billions of objects flying through ever expanding space at the speed of light, crashing into one another or struggling to form galaxies or at least patterns—all the while budding and growing or budding and exploding.

I am personally glad to know how things work and look Out There, but I am an Earthling. My society has spent uncounted billions to get us whizzing about in space and plans to spend billions more while the beauties and mysteries of our rare—maybe unique—planet wilt, shrivel and perish.

The other day I read of a young man who wanted to do great things in science but did not want to be called a scientist!

Can homo sapiens be on the right track? That is one of the questions our adventures appear to answer. In the negative.

SANDY

Our adventures! How marvelous they are! None have ever been alike. None could ever have been anticipated. So once again Rusty and I decided we must meet for some concentrated working days. To quote Lewis Carroll's *Through the Looking Glass*:

> "The time has come," the walrus said,
> To talk of many things:
> Of shoes and ships and sealing wax—
> Of cabbage and kings—And why the sea is boiling
> hot
> And whether pigs have wings."

In other words it was time to start organizing our bits and pieces into a manuscript—a mighty job that excluded, alas, the temptation of a trip.

We regretfully gave up meeting in an exciting new city and Rusty came to Savannah, my home base, where it was convenient for me at a busy time and there would be small chance of being distracted. Do I hear you snorting, Melanie?

It started of course at once. The only reservation possible for the four days was at an inn with which I was not familiar.

I met Rusty at the airport and we drove to the inn, a restored four-story castle of red brick and white stone with turrets and balconies, gables and a captain's walk. The lady at the desk welcomed us by name, personally took us upstairs to one of the most charming rooms I have ever seen, introduced us to a delightful floor maid called Clementine, and went to bring ice tea and cakes.

"I'm Clementine," said Clementine unnecessarily. "I'll do everything to make you comfortable. I hope you girls won't mind that you are in a haunted room. It's the only room in the inn with twin beds. She only comes when there are two ladies or two gentlemen, never a couple. She's very nice, actually, as she only puts an arm around your shoulders."

"Doors of the wardrobe will open and bang and shades go up after you've closed them for the night and sometimes there's whistling on the third floor," she went on. "Let me know if you need anything."

The old house was furnished in exquisite taste. Our room was both elegant and pixilated—deep blue and white wallpaper, deep blue patterned rug, blue flowers on the marble mantel, also a blue plate with a quail (one of the symbols of Artemis). The beds were covered with heavy, blue chenille spreads and blue bolsters.

"I have never felt so completely at home or so wildly excited," I said as we started to unpack. "My God!"

Rusty had pulled from her suitcase a pair of electric blue shoes, so electric and so blue and so unlike Rusty that I was silenced. Out came a pair of blue slacks only slightly more subdued.

"It's really not like me," she admitted, "but aren't they great? I simply had to have them." We sat on the beds and stared at one another. With a rush of familiar understanding we knew what was happening.

There was no time to work that afternoon, so we went for a walk. Rusty wore her bright blue shoes.

We must have seen 16 electric blue automobiles, three tourist busses banded by stripes of the same color. In the window of an ancient lock and key shop, almost invisible beneath cobwebs, padlocks, keys and Coca-Cola bottles, was a faded print of "The Blue Boy" by Thomas Gainesborough.

We went back to the house by way of a side street and just at the corner of the inn, scratched deeply into the cement of the sidewalk, was the word BLUE.

Blue was being presented to us with, perhaps, more insistence that any other symbol that we could remember. It was everywhere—in every inch of our room and wherever we went for the four days.

When we live these experiences they are more real than conventional reality and our understanding of them is clear and firm. The symbols and subsequent revelations are always comprehensible sooner or later. In recording this, I am not trying to be convincing, I am just writing down what happens.

At breakfast at the beginning of the first full day, the manager appeared, told us she had heard that we were here to work and had arranged for us to use an attic room that would be free and give us space.

What a room! It was the size of the whole top floor with strange odd unfinished rafters and a ladder to the captain's walk which was roped off.

In weird contrast, the furniture was exquisite—lovely antiques. There were also huge bunches of tall, dried flowers, strange screens telling inexplicable tales, and Indian pots. We worked at a long table complete with ice water and a special telephone. Clementine said to be sure not to use the bathroom as it was haunted most of the time and the lights would go off and on.

The whole room was so charged and electric that even the air conditioner faltered. We worked like souls possessed and finished everything we came to do and more in three mornings.

In a way we had been anxious that if we pulled everything together we might arrive at some kind of climax, and therefore the end of You-and-I, meaning no more adventures. Such a thought was unthinkable, but we knew it was possible. Now we knew it was not.

The last morning, after dutifully finishing every scrap of work we had come to do we took off for luncheon. We then had one of the convoluted, unmistakable, impossible adventures only Hermes could have contrived.

The temperature was in the 90s, so for the first time we took my car. The restaurant we had chosen was closed. On a Thursday? I suddenly thought of another place that had been recommended. Nowhere to park. Wider and wider circles. Finally, there was a vacant spot at the side of the Telfair Museum. After getting out and locking the car we noticed a sign that announced that this was private parking for Telfair visitors. It also announced that all violators would be towed away to some undecipherable address by Bubba Parker. We went into the museum to get a visitor's permit to foil Bubba Parker, and there was our revelation and our reassurance.

But first I must go back to something that happened during the trip to Myrtle Beach—something that seemed unimportant at the time. It was when the strange cloud shadow without a cloud had followed Rusty on the beach. We had gone to a library, as she has written, to do research on clouds and had joyfully learned about Cloud Cuckoo Land. We observed the Greek word for cloud is nephos and that there was a stone called nephrite—a cloudy form of jade symbolic of longevity.

We had from then on tucked in the back of our minds a hope that one day we would discover nephrite but never did.

In the Telfair Museum, for this one week only, there was

an exhibition of contemporary Chinese sculpture. The pieces were all carved of either jade or nephrite. The whole exhibition was beautiful, but for us two pieces will never, never be forgotten.

In the center of the room was an amazing, exquisitely carved serpent and across from it a strange bowl shaped like a bird. In the bowl lay two small human figures. It was labeled PROTECTIVE PHOENIX SHELTER. Both were carved in nephrite.

The next day we parted. Rusty, who rarely forgets anything, forgot her electric blue shoes. When she called to thank me for mailing them to her, she read to me what she had found in her rare library.

BLUE: air, heaven, sea, the abode of the gods, eternity, constancy, coolness, courage, freedom, glory, happiness, hope, serenity, tenderness, truth, sublimity, and contrariwise: coldness, cruelty, despair, destruction, inconstancy, merciless justice. Connected to the circle, the moon, the subconscious. The Great Serpent who represented eternal wisdom was blue. We had already discovered that serpents are androgynous symbols, but Rusty found more stuff in a new book.

SERPENT: androgyny, circle, divine emanation, guardianship, health, intelligence, pleasure, power, prophecy, the unfathomable, wisdom, and contrariwise: death, deceit, destruction, evil, grief, materialism, revenge, sin, treachery and worldliness.

The symbols of blue and serpent went on for pages as they seem to be the ultimate symbols of the opposites, androgyny. They encompass all "good" and all "evil."

Rusty also told me, and I didn't doubt it for a moment, that she and her husband had that morning found a snake in the upper floor of her house. A serpent in the upper floor of a house in New Hampshire when it was still cold outside?

And speaking of serpents, how could we both have forgotten to mention what happened at the Four Seasons Hotel in Boston? It wasn't too long ago after all—on one of those days between my summer family visits.

Rusty arrived to meet me.

The Four Seasons must be the most expensive hotel in Boston. We love it even though it now sneers at the wonderful and much more beloved old Ritz Carlton. Anyway, we decided to treat ourselves to a huge, famous Four Seasons brunch.

I do so rejoice in the trappings of a splendid brunch in a splendid expensive hotel—spotless linen, napkins placed in your lap, chairs drawn out with a bow, fresh flowers, ice tea with cut lemons in restrictive cheese cloth. I am always tempted to spill or hiccup or faint to see what the waiters would do but never, never have.

Be all that as it may, the seafood buffet was beyond anyone's dreams. On a decorated, frosty ice bed lay clams, oysters and mussels; shrimp with sauces; caviar with chopped egg, onion and lemon; an immense cold salmon; steamed fish, raw fish, lobster and crabs; rainbow trout and tuna. Everything was garnished with raw vegetables and watercress. There was, of course, every sauce imaginable.

We filled our plates and went back for more. Waiters hovered. Tea replenished, new jackets for the lemons.

Eventually I sat back replete, but took one more look at my plate in case I had missed something. I had.

Traveling between the discarded shells on my white plate was an inch long, orange-pink, transparent serpent. One end tapered to a pointed tail. On the other end was a snake's head, bullet shaped, with two bright eyes.

I don't think I will ever enjoy anything as much as holding up my hand to attract the attention of the head waiter. His face became quite pale as he looked down and then over his shoulder to see if any of the patrons had noticed a serpent crawling along the oyster shells on madam's plate.

Other dignitaries were discreetly sent for. We never got above the sous-chef, who announced it was an oyster worm. I said that I came from Georgia, had had my share of oysters and had never beheld any such worm.

The sous-chef, however, was a bit of all right. As he bore off the serpent on a clean white dish, I said, "Don't you hurt him."

"Madam," he replied, "I shall deposit him in the harbor on my way home."

When I returned to Georgia I called the Marine Institute of the University of Georgia and described our serpent to the oceanographer.

I was informed that the creature is genus *Dolichogloffuf* and species *Kowalevski*, and when mature measures 39.4 inches.

RUSTY

Looking back on my anti-science blast, I feel that I phrased the end as if it were a denouement, but there isn't any denouement; there's just more light to shed. So here goes:

Science is part of human life. How things work and what

the whole kit and kaboodle is up to are human obsessions. Science proffers a myriad of answers, some fascinating, some horrendous, but every one partial. They're far more reliable than theological answers (and much less likely to produce bloodshed), but they don't tell all.

Do you remember the Danny Kaye song that your grandmother and I used to sing to you children?

> Inchworm measuring,
> Measuring the marigolds,
> Seems to me you'ld stop and see
> How beautiful they are.

Otherness suffuses everything. Life does not surrender all its secrets to measurement or manipulation, nor can it be held in a laboratory nor captured within the walls of any "house of worship."

We have to be aware, Melanie, or maybe it's clearer to say in a state of awareness—knowing that Otherness pervades existence, that it can (and occasionally does) reach us but in a form totally unexpected and with a result that could not possibly be anticipated.

The older I get, the more I am persuaded that the natural world is the basic whereabouts of Otherness. The modern John Muir spoke of the priesthood of trees. Anyone, he felt, who spent long, silent periods among great trees would realize that they are conduits, passing on what is right and necessary to lesser woodland denizens. Ancient thinkers and dreamers were persuaded that each and every natural wonder—lake and sea, prairie and mountain, planet and star—was suffused with spirit. And there was another insight pervasive in ancient times and now largely lost to us—the link joining forms of life. People of long ago knew perfectly well that men and women aren't wandering around with eagle heads or fish tails. The half human, half non-human paintings and sculpture say, "Behold, we are all linked." Modern biology makes the same statement, but in a different tense—we were all linked, by what they call evolution. And here is something intriguing:

Darwin's idea of evolution was not the one now universally accepted, at least by laymen. He did not see creatures marching along a predestined path toward a "higher" goal—or indeed any goal at all. What he saw was change, an endless transformation from this form to that form, a happening so clear to the people of antiquity that they translated it into words, stone and paint. This "not knowing exactly what will happen next" is—or seems to us—the essence of our relationship to Hermes and without doubt one of his greatest gifts to us.

There is a point to all this, Melanie. Your aging ancestresses want you (and the others) to see what our minds have seized upon and what our adventures have validated.

Ancient people—most particularly the Greeks—observed creatures both human and non-human much as we do but interpreted them differently. Their philosophical conclusions, (regularly misunderstood by moderns) led them to embrace polytheism. Living things are both linked and individual. They differ and yet are all suffused with Otherness of some kind. Gods fit into this scheme. One God does not.

SANDY

"Here's something to think about," Rusty phoned one day when she was laboring on this opus. "We sketch—very lightly—contacts made here and there, but for the most part this whole thing reads like a tale of two people yards high surrounded by Lilliputians—and colorless ones at that. Should we do something about this?"

So we did.

We further raised the income of AT&T (one of our dedicated pursuits) until we settled on four people memories—two apiece: one dealing with long ago and one with just the other day. Rusty said she would start.

RUSTY

Here is my first:

It was December in New York, the afternoon following a snowstorm. Granted that New York was a lot cleaner (and safer) in the early 40s than it is nowadays, still this day was so brilliant and so welcoming that we knew it was a special You-and-I day, ripe for special adventure.

We decided to go to Greenwich Village where neither of us had ever been—Sandy because she was brought up in Michigan and I because I was brought up in a Victorian household which, though situated in New York, dwelt in the 19th century as to time.

A lot of people find the song "White Christmas" revoltingly treacly, but not me. On this day it soared forth from cars, public buildings and arm-in-arm strollers. There were some shiny new and extremely odd little vehicles that chugged about heaping up snow here and there. And there was a feeling of warmth in the cold, sparkling air, which we had come to realize was War Warmth.

World War II was undoubtedly the last to have this quality. It was very far from being the last war, 127 having been fought between 1945 and 1989, (just ask the United Nations if you don't believe me), but it was the last where Good and Evil showed up plain as day. Almost everyone wanted to help. Warmth spread like light and everyone talked to everyone. We reached the Village at mid-day but we couldn't leave. We dined in a tiny bistro and then wandered a bit, urging one another to hail a taxi and go.

And then we heard Dixieland, pouring from a corner night-clubbish looking spot with NICK'S gleaming above the door.

We longed, yearned, died to go in but weren't quite sure.

"Hi! Want to come in with us?"

There stood two soldiers about our age, enlisted men but very spiffily starched and pressed, with the sort of wide, enthusiastic smiles that must have been plastered upon the faces of Sandy and Rusty.

Why not?

So in we went.

Sandy was a Dixieland enthusiast, but I wasn't—well, I didn't know anything about Dixieland. In about two minutes I was spellbound. That music went right through me—through all four of us, I guess. It was an experience—of dancing (though we were all sitting down) and of laughing and rejoicing—but something else as well. I seem to remember being taken over, occupied—and Sandy says that's how she recalls this too. The musicians, we discovered, were famous and I'm sure that was part of it, but only a part. Hermes (still known as the Cosmics) was unquestionably there, gladdened along with us.

The soldiers were sculptors dedicated, even passionate, on the subject. Their joy in the music and the whole adventure matched ours. In the occasional musical silences we communicated, talking in the way we sometimes can with strangers, not wasting a moment on small-talk, just plunging right in. They understood us instantly—and we them. Their faces shone with reflected magic and clearly ours did too.

They had an idea they were going to the Far East, maybe just because for some reason they wanted to, but whatever befell them through the years, for us they're forever at that scratched-up table in that dim, smoky, enchanted dive.

And now here is my second memorable memory, though it's terribly hard to choose. There are so many:

We were in Palm Beach, settled in a relative's apartment suddenly and delightfully offered to us. We walked on the famous beach, which turned out to be just a pleasant, rather narrow stretch—nowhere near as spectacular as the wide, wild stretch on Sandy's island. We stared at the famous houses of famous millionaires (or possibly billionaires) and thought how crowded and paltry they looked compared to the Old World palaces and castles of once-upon-a-time millionaires. And then we walked down and up and down the streets.

Well, there was plenty of stuff that plutocrats could pick up for a song like a change purse the size, shape, color and design of half an orange—price $500. There were also galleries, strings of them on both sides of the streets. The paintings of the moment were all huge, with snicker-snack brush-work in colors that leapt at you with loud shouts. And then, out of the blue as always, Hermes appeared—three dimensionally and in plain sight this time.

A replica of the famous Mercury/Hermes statue (the one in the National Gallery, the one in the garden in Charleston that captivated us the Day of the Mockingbird) stood just inside the open door of an art store. In the window were the usual blaring canvases with snicker-snack brush-work. The contrast between a detailed Renaissance bronze and the abstract in the window was enough to lure us in even if the statue had not been Hermes. But that's who it was all right, solid in matter and volatile in essence, body and soul.

A large untidy man with a shock of dark hair peered at us from a large untidy desk. "Why the statue?" we asked as one.

He shrugged. "The boss likes it," he said. "It keeps him going in the middle of all this crap. Keeps me going too."

"Then the crap isn't yours?" Sandy asked.

"God Almighty, NO," he shouted.

"Then what are you doing here?"

As you can perceive, we knew this man after a few seconds. This is what can happen with You-and-I.

"I'm just here to answer questions about the crap," he grinned. "And what I get for it is space of my own in back."

"Can we see?"

He stared at us, nodded, locked the door, put up a CLOSED sign and led us through a maze into his own private showroom.

His paintings were small, polished, exquisite. Buildings seemed to dominate the canvases—roof tops, walls, gateways, corridors. At first glance it was the delicate and beautifully controlled technique that captured the eye—but that first glance only lasted a moment. The scenes were of old places, but to "how old" and "where located" and "why" there were no answers. Figures appeared here and there, strolling or perhaps peering or hiding. Or escaping? A small child stood on a chair in space way, way above the rooftops, reaching for the moon.

We looked at the paintings. We looked at the artist. He looked at us. We sat on creaky chairs and talked. And talked and talked. Time as usual had no reality. The CLOSED sign was in place, the painter's job in jeopardy—and we talked some more. What about? Yearning, reaching into space, Hermes, androgyny, the mystery of sneezes, laughter, the presence of Something Other.

We had to leave. Daylight was fading. As naturally as breathing he hugged us, one after the other, and a second time for good measure.

SANDY

My turn. There is nothing so heady as flood-lit, instant approval. It's irresistible! As Rusty has written, we never saw it as harassment. There were no strings attached. I have been smiling about the last time. I certainly assume it was the last time! My God, we were in our 70s!

We stayed at a glamorous hotel, explored and laughed and talked the daylight hours away. Almost every evening before going out for dinner, we had a cocktail in the bar. I can see plainly a large, long, charming room with high wicker-backed chairs and ceiling fans. There was, in the corner, a modest piano and a modest piano player.

Our song, "You-and-I," has long been forgotten and the marvelous orchestras of the 1940s are only heard on recordings. Our piano player had never heard of it, but the very next night, bless him, he had unearthed the old music and played it as we came into the room. It was joyous.

Our last night I shall not forget. It is always a special night and we were late coming down for our drink, as we had dressed carefully (avoiding a too close mirror inspection).

We came down the stairs, and as we passed the piano our friend called, "I'm so glad you came. You light up the room." He then softly played "You-and-I."

How is it possible? But there's more.

In a glow we ordered our vodka martinis with a twist. Not long after, a youngish man approached our table. We had noticed four men sitting nearby.

"You are amazing," he said. "You are *ladies*—but you *sparkle*."

An hour later, the head of the music department in a university out west had heard all about my island, Rusty's books and lectures and about You-and-I. Finally his wife appeared, not too happy about being abandoned in their room. The spell was broken.

But, as he left for dinner with his wife, he turned back, fell upon his knees in the cocktail bar of the hotel and kissed our hands. As we had promised, when we got home we sent him our books and he sent us tapes of his music.

On our last day we had lunch at a very special little French restaurant. We were sad of course, as it was the end of another trip. As we went to the cashier to pay our bill, a most attractive man with a noticeable French accent leapt from his chair, came over to Rusty, and bowed.

"It was so wonderful to look at you, madame," he said.

***

And now for a memory from long ago:

Remembering and writing, writing and remembering is a joy. Remembering is like a golden flash, as sharply bright as ever. And writing You-and-I memories flows without thinking, like a waterfall.

Today a happening flashed so clearly across my mind that I just closed my eyes and watched the whole incredible thing unwind.

We were in Montreal at the gorgeous old hotel which wasn't called *grand* but could have been because it truly was—and is. Our families had stayed there for generations and Rusty and I had managed it from time to time when we could find the cash.

Before we left on this trip and while en route, we talked about one of the many ideas that had been thrust upon us over and over again. Things are not what they seem. A certain object or fact is always the same but can appear totally different depending on the person looking at it.

We touched idly on the old saw about beauty being in the eye of the beholder and then we began to get into it. Might we, for instance, have differing reactions to beauty? To a tree? The sea? Lions? Probably not. How about people? A man? And we were off.

It was fun and silly, but absorbing. We considered and

argued, starting out from quite different points of view. But finally he appeared in our minds, clear as dawn.

He was tall and fit. Rusty said he had smoothly muscular arms and legs (she is a ballet freak). I insisted on black, very rich, springy hair. Rusty saw a wide, curved mouth with the corners tucked in and an aquiline, high-bridged nose. I saw dark and thick eyelashes and eyebrows and brown eyes with golden glints.

Arrived at our destination, we were greeted with a flourish, registered with a flourish and, with a flourish, ushered into the polished brass and mahogany elevator. The doors discreetly closed—almost.

A hand intervened, the doors parted and there he was.

Since he was not naked, Rusty had to give up on his arms and legs, but otherwise there he stood—in every detail.

He wore a brownish tweed jacket, blue shirt, khaki pants and a strange dark red tie with what looked like a pattern of flamingos. He carried a brief case and a handsome leather overnighter.

It was a shock. Shuddering. Rusty's face was white. Mine was probably blue. When the elevator stopped, the man got out while the porter fussed with our luggage, walked down the hall, unlocked the door of Room 127 and disappeared inside.

We were deposited in a room farther down the hall in a state of collapse. How could this happen? How could one conjure up a being and then meet it? How could an hallucination appear exactly the same to two people? Were we going mad?

It was long after midnight when we decided to take a bold step. The only piece of paper available was a sheet of my stationery, which was white with a dark blue border.

"Please help us solve a mystery," we wrote. "We will be in the breakfast room at eight-thirty in the morning and will explain." We crept down the hall to room 127 and slid the sheet under the door. Restless and worried, we passed the night hours.

In the breakfast room at eight thirty we ordered but couldn't eat, our eyes fastened on the door.

At 8:35 a man entered. He wore a brownish tweed jacket, blue shirt, khaki pants. His tie was strange—a dark red with what looked like a pattern of flamingos. In his hand was a sheet of white note paper with a dark blue border.

He was heavy set, heavy faced, grey-haired—dull, dull, dull.

He searched the room in vain. He caught no eye.

From the vantage point of many years, Rusty is certain whom we conjured up and begs me to put my mind to it. I try but my mind slithers to a stop, ponders – and escapes.

Chapter 3

RUSTY

Well, here we go again—or rather, there we went.

In typical fashion we knew nothing about the new path we were now to tread. Out of the blue a godchild sent me a book about labyrinths. Why, of course, is the question we no longer bother with. I read the book, sent it on to your grandmother and presto—we were off. I knew it at once and so did she.

As always, I clawed my way through the bibliography and sent for various books about labyrinths, one from Cornell—very heavy and as dull as only respected scholars can make an exciting subject—and several just the opposite. One of the latter came from my godchild, others from the library of the American Society of Dowsers.

A labyrinth is not a maze, though its form is similar. A maze is a trick where for amusement—or possibly punishment—you are quickly lost. In a labyrinth you cannot get lost. Every pathway in leads to the heart. Every pathway out leads back to the entrance.

I read on and on, sometimes slogging, sometimes dancing and then, abruptly, the heart of the matter emerged.

The most famous labyrinth of all time was Cretan, possibly underground and probably make-believe. By now it is so encrusted with legends that it is impossible to tell. Minos, King of Crete, was enormously powerful. Even Athens was at his beck and call – to such an extent that every year seven Athenian youths and seven Athenian maidens were sent to Crete to be devoured by a monster known as the minotaur. He was kept in a labyrinth so cleverly constructed that everyone who attempted to enter and slay the minotaur became the minotaur's dinner instead.

Nonetheless, Theseus, son of the Athenian king, determined to give it a try. Fortunately for Theseus, Ariadne, daughter of Minos, took one look at him and fell in love. She gave the young hero a ball of string so he could get all the way in, kill the horrible creature and get all the way out. Before Minos could erupt in what would surely have been an explosive rage, Theseus fled with his 13 Greek companions and Ariadne to the island of Naxos.

Apparently 15 was a good number for a fiesta, so Ariadne led them in the crane dance, whose back and forth steps not only mimic the crane's mating pattern, but are said to create the outline of a seven circuit labyrinth. It is sad to relate that Theseus lightheartedly abandoned his princess on the isolated island and dashed off in search of more adventures.

However, as you may recall if your mind hasn't wandered, the god Dionysus not only rescued her but married and immortalized and remained faithful to her.

If you can't quite pick up all these sticks and lay them straight, Melanie, don't fret. It's that wonderful recurring last line that lights it all up: THE CRANE WAS A BIRD SACRED TO THE ROMAN MERCURY AND THE GREEK HERMES.

Well, there we were—a totally fabulous situation presenting itself as always, and again as always, insisting that we do something. Needless to say, the where and when promptly showed up. A seminar was set for the first week of August on the campus of a small college in northern Vermont—almost at the Canadian border. We made a reservation at a motel, enrolled in the seminar and chomped at the bit until the magic day arrived.

A three-hour drive brought us to the proper area but not the proper town—this despite the fact that our driver (we're too ancient to undertake such an excursion with either of us at the wheel) claimed to know the area well. This of course was a classic Hermes touch.

We wandered and wandered and finally, at the moment of despair, arrived at our destination. The motel was a few yards from the highway and unprepossessing. Our hearts sank—and promptly rose when we discovered a huge, charming room (and big bathroom) faced away from the road and spotless. Directly beside us was a dreary looking restaurant which nonetheless produced first class cordon bleu food, fine service and smiling faces.

SANDY

When Rusty sent me the book about labyrinths, my ancient heart stopped beating and the room spun. At that time I really knew nothing about labyrinths but once again—yes, once again—I was sick with excitement.

Nowadays each adventure we have is obviously the last. How could we have more to learn? How can we survive another wild adventure? But, of course, there was more to learn, we did survive and it was a wild adventure.

As Rusty has written, the seminar took place on the campus of a small college in northern Vermont. Ours was a branch of a much larger conference on dowsing.

The first morning we went into the main building to register and there on our left was a table sparkling with agates, quartz, jasper, crystal and other small stones. A sign over them read, “Please take two stones. If you take more the dowsers will know.” We were tempted but obedient.

Our classroom was smallish with wooden school chairs, a blackboard and a front desk. There were 12 of us and two teachers.

A rotund, greying, jolly man, one of the two, asked us to introduce ourselves. There was a witch from Florida, a father with two adult sons, an ersatz shaman, barefooted swathed in blue and green draperies, a weird person who looked more like a witch than the witch. The other four were too normal to remember. Since Rusty had made the initial registration, our name tags were both Pool and we immediately became the Pool girls. Girls?

All morning the rotund gentleman told us stories about

labyrinths—all rather boring. His approach was dull and embarrassingly cute at times.

For luncheon we ate pimento cheese sandwiches and drank Sprite in the school cafeteria.

But in the afternoon we built a real true labyrinth in the football field. Rather, they did. We watched. It was scorching hot, no shade, beaten down grass. It took two hours. I barely remember a haze of earnest and dedicated fat bottoms crawling about with measuring tapes.

At last it was finished—a classical seven-circuit earth labyrinth, marked out by stakes jammed into the parched ground.

We were ready for our first spiritual experience.

Shoeless and sockless, holding sweaty hands and chanting some earthy sound, we danced our very first labyrinth path staggering with heat exhaustion, bumping into thin stakes of wood that somehow rang bells. It was ghastly.

Eventually we reached the center, where one is supposed to pause, gather arcane energy or something that had not been made clear to us. We were jammed together in a space the size of a dining room table, bosom to bosom.

No one that I could see had a spiritual experience. Subsequently no one knew what to do. In desperation, one of the older man's adult sons gathered himself together and told a remarkably dirty joke and after a pause we all danced back to the entrance.

Rusty and I knew we simply could not leave it like that and decided to wait until everyone had gone and then walk the path by ourselves. But no, the fake shaman waited too, and got there first.

She danced and chanted and kissed the earth and in the

center she gathered her blue and green draperies between her legs and stood on her head. Rusty and I went back to the hotel.

The next day was another story altogether. Our teacher was a charming, articulate and dedicated woman. Her descriptions of the use of the labyrinth and its history were remarkable and exciting. Rusty and I started to feel the wonder that we had anticipated.

In the afternoon our teacher laid out the 11 circuit Chartres Cathedral labyrinth. It was a huge canvas laid in sections, lined in a lovely purple and spaced with candles and flowers. It seemed so inappropriate in a school gymnasium instead of in the outdoors that Rusty suggested we each pretend we had an animal with us. Everyone agreed and our leader said, "We will be led by our elders, the Pool girls."

The Pool girls were touched and our walk was silent and happy. I had a very different feeling during the half hour it took to walk this labyrinth. When I reached the center I felt my old dog, Sheppie, with me and I tried not to cry.

Our trip was far from what we had expected yet the idea of the labyrinth itself was profound. So deep was it that we knew that we must have one of our very own. Rusty discovered the name of a man whose work it was to build labyrinths—and thereby hangs our tale.

RUSTY

He was in human form, but was clearly an elf or sprite or maybe part hobbit. His hair was white his eyes aquamarine and his ears pointed. I had located several spots suitable (I thought) for a labyrinth. None of them was acceptable, but he did linger over my first choice. It was (and is) a tree.

For many years I had watched with amazement a tiny oak which was struggling to grow—or even live—at the foot of a giant spruce. Since the spruce was in a field, several yards from the forest edge, there was plenty of space for another tree. Why was this little creature pressed against a giant, roots presumably entangled? I became involved with the curious and somehow moving drama.

Finally, the ancient spruce began to die. I hate to fell great trees and so does my family, but we had it brought down lest it fall. The tree men carted it away, leaving a huge stump—and a tiny stranger which almost instantly began to grow. It grew like a fountain shooting into the air. In a short time, casual observers remarked, "I don't remember an oak over there." As it grew (and it is now almost as tall as the old spruce) it developed in a peculiar fashion—peculiar, that is, for an oak. It became like a dancer with spread skirts.

My elfin builder stared for a while at my leafy dancer but did not stay. After trudging over an extensive area, he suddenly said, "Here!"

I was staggered. The chosen spot was under "Sylvia's tree," a vast old maple where my daughter (who died some years ago) spent much of her childhood.

"Why?" I asked, trying to keep my voice steady.

"Just because," he replied, but then he said something else.

"That tree of yours. It's not the right place for your labyrinth, but there's something about it. Let's go back there."

He gazed at the tree, then smiled ear to ear and clasped his hands. "It's a girl," he stated, "a beautiful young girl.

But oak trees are never female. They're always masculine and always regal—in fact, they are the king of trees. This is strange."

So of course I sat him down on the spruce stump and attempted in elfin terms to tell the tale of androgyny. He appeared to be listening, but I sensed he wasn't. It just all slid over his elfin head.

"You must offer her gifts," he presently told me. "There must always be something here for her—here on the stump."

I haven't found too many things yet and don't want to make a mistake. I think about it while I walk my labyrinth.

SANDY

I fretted and yearned when I came back to my island. I even picked the perfect place. It is called the Peter Pan Pond. When my house was built in 1926 a curving pond was made. We had artesian wells then and it was full of clear water. A cement Peter Pan stands on a mossy mound at one end and on the side Tinker Bell lies on her stomach, her chin in her hands. Trees are everywhere and azaleas, wisteria, dogwood and, at Christmas and Easter, narcissus, snowdrops and day lilies.

But I had no way of cutting the intricate pattern of a large labyrinth. Then one day walking through the woods with three young friends I told them the history of the labyrinth and added the adventures that Rusty and I had had at the seminar. They were excited and longed to build a labyrinth for me and so set to work. I had a diagram of a seven-circuit labyrinth which I pinned on a tree and from that we were able to measure and create the intricate pathway.

Under an oak tree we found a pile of Savannah Grey handmade bricks—the ruins of a forsaken building. Placed lengthwise on their sides, they perfectly border the path.

The path is beautiful, changing with the seasons, covered with wisteria and day lilies, then green grasses, then brown oak leaves. It is just right. I share it with my animals. Today I walked it with my son, a horse, a dog, a cat, two peacocks and a duck.

The bricks, so easily overturned, are seldom disturbed. Sometimes one or two are knocked over by an armadillo or a wild pig rooting for acorns, but they are easily set straight.

So far my walks to the center and back have given me quiet and a needed remoteness. Almost always, animals come with me. And I think of the dancing cranes.

RUSTY

Then there was a unique trip to Charleston. The trip was unique because we couldn't go where we had planned to go.

We had long ago become accustomed to frustrations of all kinds, from small losses to large misapprehensions. Never, however, had we been completely blocked from reaching our destination. Sandy chose Thomasville, Ga., as our destination and tried to get reservations for a time convenient to us both. No soap. Why Thomasville? Who knows, except Hermes?

Finally accepting a not-so-good-but-still-possible period, we set to work altering this and that and getting things squared away. At the last minute I got sick—very sick—with some kind of horrendous bug picked up on a horrendous 16-hour airplane flight. There followed the usual maddening change of reservations and tickets. Well I recovered, again got everything squared away, was practically on the way to the airport when Sandy fell ill. This time we just gave up on Thomasville, cancelling the whole thing.

Twenty four hours later, Sandy completely recovered. So we decided to go to Charleston. Things always work out in Charleston. Of course there was all the usual "Sorry, madam, we have no rooms available…oh, wait a moment, we've just had a cancellation" business that defines a Hermes trip.

We walked the old beloved streets, visiting the old beloved spots, beginning, as always, with the Clowns' Bazaar. Alas, Sister is no longer, but her dearest friend Ms. Wagoner is still among us. We gazed upon the pixilated treasures amassed from around the world (to help the creative indigent) and, as always, could not resist a bit here and a bit there. And, greater joy, we talked about Sister, a staid-and-proper nun who made exquisite religious objects with a twist. Somewhere there was always a bit of ribbon or a gum-drop or something tiny and unlikely or something upside down—a hermetic figure if ever there was one.

And then a mockingbird found us and stayed with us, flying from pole to pole and roof-top to roof-top. All the way to the garden with the bronze Mercury—and there he was in all his splendor. Had he been absent, I cannot imagine what would have become of us.

But so far, though H. was clearly with us, nothing new had occurred. And then of course it did.

All tizzied up, we set forth for one of the Charleston restaurants. We had never been there before—just picked the name out of a hat. At a street corner, Sandy grabbed my arm and announced loud and clear that "In one moment we're going to come upon something."

Sure enough, hidden in a beautiful garden, probably unseen by nine out of ten passers-by, a unicorn lay in a flower bed. At the end of the street was our restaurant.

We opened the door and were stunned by a row of huge birds—huge—made of something odd, maybe a kind of wicker. "They're quite something, our cranes, aren't they?" remarked a chipper young waitress.

When Sandy got home, she was met by five solar energy men, one a bird expert who had been working at the other end of her island. They were almost speechless but managed to sputter out the information that they had just seen four Sand Hill cranes in the marsh, gorgeous creatures tall as the men's shoulders. Never, ever, had these birds been seen there before.

Chapter 4

SANDY

A hermaion, as we have learned some time ago, is a gift of Hermes. It is also, as I recall, a lucky find. Sometimes I think that maybe the greatest of Hermes' gifts to us is how to recognize these treasures. Lucky finds—or chances and accidents with double meanings—are around us always. They are part of creation. Hermes has taught us to see them. Common events become uncommon. Imaginable—and even unimaginable—things and thoughts come into focus.

And of course a related hermaion—or maybe another side of the same one—is the perpetual underlining of something he taught us long ago. Mischief and laughter are boon companions of weighty matters. Upside always has a down.

How absolutely marvelous it all is! How overwhelmingly exciting that year after year and decade after decade we continue to revel in such an adventure!

It seems to me that what fell recently into Rusty's lap is a first-class hermaion—three mind-blowing books. I've read the two she sent me. (She says she'll cope with the third as a sort of Grande Finale.) The whole thing strains my powers of belief, but I'll do the best I can.

Book One: *Hermes: Literature, Science, Philosophy*, by Michel Serres, edited by Joshe Harari and David Bell.

The blurb on the jacket starts with a quote from René Girard, Stanford University:

> By all criteria of intelligent opinion and current visibility, Michel Serres is one of the two or three most powerful figures in French intellectual circles today. In a very simplified manner, one might say that Serres always runs counter to the prevalent notion of the two cultures—scientific and humanistic—between which no communication is possible. In Serres's words, 'criticism is a generalized physics,' and whether knowledge is written in philosophical, literary or scientific language it nevertheless articulates a common set of problems that transcends academic disciplines and artificial boundaries.

Michel Serres, the blurb continues, has built a reputation as one of modern France's most original and important thinkers. His unique view of the world of knowledge, based upon his explorations of the parallel developments of scientific, philosophical and literary trends, has provided the basis for numerous books, including the five-volume *Hermes* series.

Serres is not in a class with Agatha Christie. In fact, if one stays awake all night, it is less from thrills than from headache. Nevertheless, I am quite set up to discover that one of France's "most original and important thinkers" not only knows Hermes but is a passionate fan. Harari and Bell in their introduction speak of Hermes' (and Serres') fluctuating between the "universality of form and the individuality of circumstances" and call the method of passage a journey. To Serres (and Hermes), they assure us, this journey is a *randonnée*, an expedition filled with "random discoveries that exploit the varieties of spaces and times."

The second hermaion book is entitled *Hermes*, *Guide of Souls* (Spring Publications, Inc., 1987), and it is by our old friend Karl Kerenyi. This book is wonderfully readable and keeps the reader awake, headacheless. The introduction (called here a prefatory note) neatly suggests what is to come. It is by Magda Kerenyi.

In a correspondence with Thomas Mann, Magda writes, Kerenyi

> ...added the Hermetic as a third configuration to the dualism of Apollonian and Dionysian which Nietsche introduced into cultural history. Kerenyi understood the Hermetic as a specific quality in the nature, achievements and life patterns of mankind, as well as of the corresponding traits of roguery to be found on the surface of man's world.

In a letter to Kerenyi, Thomas Mann wrote: "Hermes, my favorite divinity," suggesting, says Magda, that these two renowned literary figures "shared a predilection for the same god."

But predilection seems too mild a word to use, at least for Kerenyi. Hermes, Magda goes on to say, was "so closely involved with his life that he recognized the continuous presence and effects of this divinity."

Magda states that Kerenyi's "special personal relation to Hermes derived from the *journey* as the essential support of his life and work." But finding and losing also belong to the ambivalent sphere of the "God of journey who so often put into Kerenyi's hand just the right reading material for a voyage. But Hermes could also reveal his presence through contrariness, as we can read in Kerenyi's diary."

In the Thai Canal, it seems, Kerenyi lost his copy of Anatole France's *Revolte des Anges*. Years later, says Kerenyi's journal, "it is precisely Anatole France…that was again stolen from me, disappeared together with the chair I had reserved…Does Hermes wish to play the same game with me again? In any event I am left with the feeling of being stolen from, something uncanny, a vague sense of change in circumstances—truly something hermetic."

Magda:

> Hermaion, a gift of Hermes, meant for Kerenyi that a book or an article unexpectedly appeared at hand in the right moment, even independently of traveling. His Hermes lecture, on August 4, 1942, played an important part in his life, quite concretely favoring a crucial journey: the appreciation of this lecture in the Swiss press facilitated permission to leave Hungary and then later to establish himself definitely in the free world. (Then began) "the difficult existence

> of the free, private scholar, although interwoven and protected by Hermes.

In a letter to Frau Hermann Hesse, dated November 11, 1942, Kerenyi wrote,

> The world of Hermes has been holding me captive ever since my lecture until the day before yesterday, and you will be amazed how much it grew and ripened since its conception in the lecture—an unexpected and passively received conception into its final, and even for myself, surprising shape.

The last paragraph in *Hermes: Guide of Souls* sums up Kerenyi's love and knowledge of his god:

> Whoever does not shy away from the dangers of the most profound depths and the newest pathways, which Hermes is always prepared to open, may follow him and reach, whether as scholar, commentator or philosopher, a greater find and a more certain possession. For all to whom life is an adventure—whether an adventure of love or of spirit—he is the common guide. Koinos Hermes!

We know this—all of it, yet to hear it from Serres and Kerenyi takes my breath away. If You-and-I had seen these writings years ago it is possible that an immediate fascination could have influenced the discovery of what was behind our unbelievable adventures with Hermes.

But we didn't find them years ago, we found them when we were ancient. We found them at the crossroads.

RUSTY

And now to Lewis Hyde and his book *Trickster Makes This World: Mischief, Myth and Art* (Farrar, Straus and Giroux, 1998)—the third book in Hermes' latest hermaion to us.

Reading this book was a thrill, a delight, a vindication. It gave me what my children used to call a slippery stomach and what the modern young call a high.

His picture on the dust cover suggests a teenager, but he has worked, we learn, as an electrician, counselor and professor. He is also a poet, a MacArthur Fellow and former director of creative writing at Harvard. At present he is Luce Professor of Art and Politics at Kenyon. This is impressive, but as far as I am concerned all that matters is that he knows Hermes—and knows him intimately.

According to Lewis, the Greek Hermes is not just a trickster, but *the* trickster, prototype, archetype, model—however you want to put it. Other societies, it seems, have their tricksters, but only if ancient ideas have somehow survived.

"Outside such traditional contexts there are no modern tricksters because trickster only comes to life in the complex terrain of polytheism. If the spiritual world is dominated by a single high god opposed by a single embodiment of evil then the trickster disappears."

According to old myths, the fly leaf informs us, "the trickster made the world as it actually is." Where other gods envisioned something more ideal—perhaps even perfect—this world "with its complexity and ambiguity, its beauty and its dirt, was trickster's creation, and the work is not yet finished."

I have read and re-read this book and with the greatest difficulty picked out quotes. My first quote foray produced 15 pages. In agony I have cut and cut until I could bear no more. So here we go.

Briefly, the trickster, according to Hyde, is the boundary crosser, the lord of in-between.

> Poised on the threshold, he is in *his* world, the crepuscular, shady, mottled, ambiguous, androgynous, neither/nor space of Hermetic operation, that thin layer of topsoil where...things are not yet differentiated. From this position Hermes can move in either direction or, more to the point, act as the agent by which others are led in either direction. (Hermes may) lead the way or lead astray.

And here is Lewis in what is undeniably the voice of Hermes—(also the voice of yours truly, who is always suspicious of The Truth):

"We may well hope our actions carry no moral ambiguity, but pretending that is the case when it isn't does not lead to clarity about right and wrong; it more likely leads to unconscious cruelty masked by inflated righteousness."

Hurray!

And one more Hydian (or Hermetic) thought on the subject of ambiguity: "Creative mobility in this world requires, at crucial moments, the strategic erasure of ethical boundaries."

Wonderful Hyde on culture is, (it should go without saying) wonderful:

Cultures regularly suffer from contingency; they bump into things they do not expect and cannot control. How much control can we have before the good life we're guarding ceases to be good in any conventual sense? Can we reduce contingency to zero, or must we always have some exposure to things we cannot control? Is the life that has no risk a human life? Nussbaum argues that "one strain of Greek thought was clearly skeptical of any impulse to order that would close out all contingency!" The good life must periodically occupy "the razor's edge of luck," they say, which means that the art of living, in Nussbaum's words, "requires the most delicate balance between order and disorder, control and vulnerability."

These are the claims that raise the hackles of all who believe in divine intention, of course. Feeling ourselves to be the center of things, and witnessing the complexity of the surrounding world, who could believe that creation arose from a series of cumulatively selected accidents? "All religion," Monod writes, "nearly all philosophies, and even a part of science testify to the unwearying, heroic effort of mankind desperately denying its own contingency"—all religions except the many that preserve a trickster figure. It is perfectly possible to have a system of belief that recognizes accident as part of creation. In Yoruba mythology, Eshu is understood to have gotten one of the creator gods drunk at the beginning of time, and that is why there are cripples, albinos and all other sorts of anomaly in the world. When geneticists breed fruit flies, a fly sometimes appears with legs growing from the sockets where its antennae ought to be. Clearly

> Eshu, who delights in mishap as well as good hap, is still slipping palm wine to the high gods.
>
> The eternals are vulnerable at their joints. Articulus can mean both a joint in the body and a turning point in the solar year. Why exactly this word has such reach becomes clear if we do a little digging in the history of Indo-European languages. Articulus belongs to a large group of related terms preserving an ancient root, *ar*, that originally meant *to join*...Many words in Greek, Latin and modern languages come from this root, all of them having to do with joining.

Many years ago Sandy and I were sitting in the Boston Ritz Bar—the old bar with crepuscular light, tricky stairs and an odd arrangement of tables (the new-and-improved bar has no meaning for us and we avoid it). Quite near us, but on a slightly different level, was a long table at which eight people were sitting. Facing us was a man of indeterminate age and features yet with a look on his face that captivated us. He was simply staring into space—not as if he were out-to-lunch but rather as if contemplating something out of sight. Conversations whizzed about him, over, around and across. Finally, someone addressed him directly. Repeating herself irritably, she attracted the attention of the other six, resulting in a sudden silence. Abruptly awakened, the dreamer looked wildly to right and left, cleared his throat and remarked loud and clear, "ar."

This word has become part of our vocabulary. We use it when bemused—for instance when one of us has missed some piece of the other's long or elaborate explication. We use it when, after adding two and two we come up with three or five, (a common occurrence on a Hermes trip), or where something so complex appears (or happens) that we cannot even begin to unravel it.

Hyde takes "ar" and all its derivations seriously. "To describe the uses of these words is to begin to sketch the unifying image I want for the work that tricksters do in regard to traps of culture." This is an "ar" moment for us, so we hasten on.

Hermes, we next discover, is the last one born among the Olympians. "By the time Hermes appears all the other gods have their prerogatives and spheres of influence; the cosmos would appear to be complete."

But it isn't. Something essential is missing.

> It is as if a human body were assembled, each of the organs duly in place...and each duly separated from the others. But what if the barriers were such that no organ could communicate with any other? Before a body can come to life, every separation, every boundary, must be breached in some way.
>
> In the Olympian case, it would appear that each of the gods has a tendency to perfect herself or himself and, in that perfecting, to solidify all boundaries. The goddess of chastity allows no licentiousness, the god of reason allows no muddle, the goddess of the hearth allows no strangers in the kitchen, the god of war allows no cowards...It is in Hades' nature to seal the gates of the underworld; no soul escapes. But when the full expression of his nature means that Persephone cannot return to earth, springtime never comes and the world begins to die. Then the gods send Hermes to bring her back.

Three cheers, four shouts and five hurrays!

And then there is the business of time. Having struggled for decades to cope with Hermes' approach to this subject, it was fascinating to read Hyde's interpretation. Hermes, he tells us, "dissolves time in the river of forgetfulness, and once time has disappeared, the eternals come forward."

Yes, they do, but to understand is definitely not the work of a moment. Hyde speaks of the "wandering crossroad mind." That puts it in a nutshell, but the more I ponder this question of mind, the more I grasp why there had to be two of us to "school it through attention." Also, as Sandy has more than once remarked, all alone the mind, however willing, might simply have blown apart.

The crossroad mind, Hyde tells us, is "generative, proliferating new structures, new symbols, new metaphors." And I came upon this with particular delight as it is always true for us: "The ingredients of such moments—surprise, quick thinking, sudden gain—suffuse them with humor."

Sooner or later, I was convinced, we would come to Picasso, and sure enough he showed up.

Hermes, as Lewis sees him, (and as we all do who are blessed with the ability to recognize his presence) is

> …neither the god of the door leading out nor the god of the door leading in—he is the god of the hinge. He is the mottled figure in the half-light, the amnigoge who simultaneously amazes and unmazes, whose wand both "bewitches the eyes of men to sleep and wakes the sleeping," as Homer says in the Iliad. I sometimes wonder if all great creative minds do not participate in this double motion, humming a new and

> catchy theogony even as they demystify the gods their elders sang about. Pablo Picasso had that double motion, disturbing classical perspective while presenting a strange new way of seeing, one so hypnotic it shows up decades after his death on billboards and children's printed pajamas.

There are so many—too many—things to say as a wind-up and anyway there is no wind-up for us nor, needless to say, for our dear and wondrous god. But a final quote from dear and wondrous Hyde will have to do. He speaks of a very special happiness, "the happiness of being released from the known and meeting the world freshly, the happiness of happenstances."

Doesn't this sound like Hermes speaking directly to Rusty and Sandy?

SANDY

Every time we try to tidy things up, pull everything together and consider the manuscript completed, something new occurs.

Rusty and I hadn't had a trip for many months and for many reasons. Rusty's husband had not been well and she couldn't leave him. I had had another attack of vertigo that, of course, involved a frightening loss of balance which is totally unpredictable and can have serious consequences. Naturally, it was diagnosed as labyrinthitis.

So far there have been no serious consequences. I have fallen downstairs four times with only one slight bump.

One time I fell down the back stairs on top of a professor of English at the University of Georgia and broke his finger. I have toppled into a fountain, a litter pan and into the same professor's bathtub. Be that as it may, Rusty and I felt that we must meet.

Rusty, as in most cases, had an idea for new research—the study of death. Why not, when it's just around the corner and has always fascinated us? She spent a month or so reading everything she could find including the writings of Plato through George Bernard Shaw.

I couldn't travel, so Rusty came to Savannah. We reserved six nights in the enchanting and enchanted inn where, a year before, we had "finished" the manuscript. Our Blue Room was the same. The wardrobe doors swung open by themselves and once there were four sharp taps on the hall door which swung open—no one there. Alas, Clementine had left.

Our first morning, as always, was spent unloading our personal horrors. How very, very special and life-saving it is to be able to do this. It is also vital in order to sweep clean the stage and raise the curtain.

In the afternoon we got to work on Death. Well, we tried, but something small and totally unimportant got in the way. It set us off and we went from small giggles to hoots and howls of helpless mirth—the rare kind that so seldom comes. We had to give up any serious pursuit.

The next day, off we set to seek, as always, deep wisdom and high adventure. Unfortunately our confident, eager stride of the past was left in the past. I was unsure and wobbly—part vertigo and part age. Rusty had a swollen leg. However, excitement and anticipation is forever.

It was a fine day but hot, hot, hot—July in Georgia. In each historic house we visited, in each shop explored, there was a deluge of our symbols—particularly blue fish, double unicorns, hares and bears. Then something happened that, even to think about, floods me with embarrassment. We fell flat in the middle of Broughton, the main street in Savannah. I lost my balance and fell face down on the pavement without a word. As I was clinging to Rusty, she came as well, landing upside down, cracking her head on the pavement, legs in the air.

Two modest, business-suited men walking behind us were smitten by the sight of two ancient ladies flailing in the street. They rushed to untangle us and haul us upright.

Never, never had we done such an outrageous thing. What bad taste!

The nice men assured themselves that there were no broken bones, propped us against a store window and left.

I had one nick on my knee the size of a quarter, and Rusty a minute knob on the back of her head. Our immaculate slacks were still immaculate. We had lunch in a small tea room back in a corner where we could try to control uncontrollable paroxysms of gut-shaking laughter. Before we left we spied two tea cups for sale complete with tea leaves in an envelope and directions on how to read them. Then back to Kehoe House. Any further exploring of Savannah was tricky, if not dangerous.

So we read our tea leaves—the kind of thing we had not done in years. Are these two scholars engaged in the study of death?

Down we settled to make the tea. Our cups were crude and squat—white with gold words around the bowl:

Spontaneity…Synchronicity…Dreams…Smiles.

We poured boiling water over the leaves, "gently twirled the cup three times." We sobered immediately as the forms thus produced were unmistakable:

Two moose (my nickname).
Boat—"A voyage in life and a transition made safely."
Bird—"Freedom and imagination."
Nest—"Safety and rest before heading out on the next journey."
Serpent—"A renewed sense of life through the irrational and ecstatic."

The rest of the afternoon was spent trying to be serious and then to harness hysteria in an expensive dinner restaurant. When we came back to the room, we found our chocolates not on our pillows, but on the bottom of upturned water glasses.

OK, Hermes. We get it. We were not approaching the subject of death properly, were we? We have been shown over and over that profound ideas and beliefs do not have to be mournful. Uncontrollable laughter is just as profound as anything else, isn't it? We can never, never avoid this, can we?

Rusty's careful notes were put away. The subject was not in our hands—or heads or philosophies.

The next morning, Rusty went out for an early walk. There is no possible way to cope with what happened, Melanie. Nonetheless, it happened.

RUSTY

I walked down Price Street simply because it was familiar and has chunks of Savannah charm. I walked all the way down to Bay Street where traffic was so intimidating that I just turned around and retraced my steps—on the same side of the street. Presently, I came upon something I had missed on the way down.

A small paved courtyard contained a giant flag pole—the tallest and thickest I have ever beheld. The pole itself would have drawn attention, but the flag was a further stunner. It was tiny—the ludicrous effect heightened by its condition. A star-spangled banner it certainly was, but in ribbons, the tip of each stripe fluttering raggedly in the breeze. A final oddity was a row of stitching all the way round the flag making the fluttering appear caught within a frame.

I don't know whether I have mentioned anywhere in these pages my huge enthusiasm for flags. I have three collections on show within the house and from time to time without—for parades or lectures.

The strange pole and its even stranger passenger was spell-binding. Presently, I lowered my eyes and further surveyed my surroundings. To my left was a low building—grey stone of no particular distinction—with a sign near the door: INTERNATIONAL PILOTS.

Directly in front of me was an iron stand topped by a bronze plaque. The exact wording now escapes me, but it was in memory of "our father" and in appreciation for all he had done for pilots. There were three names—a daughter and two sons—Elizabeth, Harris and Berg.

Since I intended to return, I studied nothing in detail,

but wanted to take one last look at the strange flag. To do so I backed across the narrow pavement and leaned against a big, old live oak. On my forehead was the word PILOT. Yes, I realize I couldn't see it. I also realize that it was not emblazoned like a scarlet letter (or more accurately a mark of Cain). Nonetheless it was there. You have to remember, Melanie, that I was on a trip with your grandmother. Nothing normal on these occasions can be counted on—in fact, nothing at all can be counted on, normal or not.

The next morning, we set off to view the weird pole and flag. I wanted Sandy to see them and also to help me decide the size of a new flag which I felt obliged to present to the International Pilots.

We walked down Price Street—all the way down. No International Pilots. We walked back. Shoulder to shoulder the houses squatted in the heat.

Sandy felt wobbly, so we returned to our mystical mansion and did some telephoning—information, tourist information, Port Authority.

"No ma'am—there's an International Company in Charleston. In Savannah though, there's only a Savannah Company." The Port Authority gave me its address—wrong street—but I tottered out anyway, found a cab and drove by the building. No connection whatsoever.

I walked once more the length of Price Street—both sides this time. I walked up and down streets on either side. Nothing. Three people asked if they could help me, so I must have looked fairly stricken. I pondered saying, "I'm looking for something that apparently isn't," but thought better of it.

"But I was there," I wailed to Sandy, back again at our house-away-from-home. "I was there."

I flopped down on my bed and thought and thought. And thought. Hermes, of course. No question about that. But saying what?

And then I saw. Hermes the psychopomp, the pilot to the Underworld, to the world we cannot find but to which he knows the pathway and possesses the key.

The rest of our trip was spent trying to digest a happening that even for us was pretty sensational. At the end of the week I felt slightly more balanced mentally and your grandmother physically. But of course I couldn't leave the adventure alone. Who on earth could?

The first thing I did when I got home was phone the International Pilots place in Charleston. The nice lady who answered obviously thought I was, to put it mildly, a little unusual, but she calmly assured me that they had no pole, no flag, no plaque. Why did I do this? Because I had the horrendous thought that I might have had an "out-of-body experience," i.e. transported (by Hermes) to Charleston as an Olympian belly laugh. The thought that this might have happened and might happen again was pretty unnerving. After a day or two of constant rumination I decided to look into the names Harris and Berg. My library produced the following:

Berg: an eminence, a mountain, a high pointed rock—also a tower.

Harris: an island in Scotland believed to be the Fortunate Isle of the ancients. "Harris" comes from *Uris,* which means great light.

Tower: deity, grandeur, sovereignty, treasure, truth, also death, also phallus. Burial place, ladder to heaven.

Fortunate Isles: also Happy Islands where the souls of

favored mortals were received by the gods and lived happily in a paradise.

Pillar: bearer of messages from a deity. White pillar—acceptance, affirmation.

I called your grandmother. In fact I called her thrice because she was so bowled over that she needed digestion time between each revelation. After Fortunate Isles and before Pillar she said, "It's all an affirmation, isn't it?" When I read the last word she asked how I now expected her to get anything ordinary done? I had no answer because I was asking myself the same question.

We always wonder how—or what—we can tell our offspring about our adventures lest they feel we've gone round the bend. This is patently absurd, because all of you have long since digested the fact that there is something about your ancestresses that suggests they are somewhat unstable, particularly when together.

Anyway, my daughter for some reason insisted that I tell her in detail about our recent excursion. When I tried just to reveal a few digestible snippets, she scoffed. So I told her the whole tale. Her comment rocked me on my heels.

"You've already had one pilot experience—that dream and then the trip to Santa Fe. You'd better watch out for a third!"

I muttered that I indeed would—but, as we might have known, what happened next was related to absolutely nothing.

It was three days before Christmas and like everybody else I had no extra time. But does time mean anything to H? No, and there can be no question that he was present.

I had begun to worry as to whether we had left anything

out of our book. Why? We don't ask that anymore.

Spiders came instantly to mind. We knew the spider was trickster of the insect world and we said so when telling about our adventures and discoveries in Sante Fe, but my thoughts stuck right there. After a restless night, I arose early, collected some breakfast and returned to bed with a tray. The temperature was 15 degrees, but we rarely have frost on our windows because we have double glass, very tight fitting. There is a window beside my bed facing east, always catching the early rays of the rising sun. The entire window was a spider web. Yes, I know that frost sometimes assumes a web-like shape. On my window was a complete work of art, slightly sagging along one edge in the manner of web recently abandoned. Spellbound in the usual hermetic fashion, I stared until, when struck directly by the sun, it slowly faded away.

I ate my breakfast, made my bed, did my boring exercises, brushed my teeth and started to turn on my bath. At the bottom of the tub was one of those big, sticky house flies that appear from nowhere in winter. I'm not enthusiastic about killing anything but draw the line at the kind of creature that creeps up walls and falls on you at night. I pressed a piece of Kleenex on the fly—hard—then lifted the corpse to dispose of it. There was no corpse on the Kleenex. There was nothing at all on the Kleenex, but racing in circles round and round the tub was a spider. I have no comment to make. Wittgenstein and Derrida, our current chief deconstructionists, are right on. Words can be both meaningless and useless.

I saw that I had injured the spider, whose sense of direction was askew along with one leg. I killed him—with profound apologies, and feel miserable. No spider has ever before died by my hand. It is to be hoped that I will not have to pay too heavily for my sin.

Needless to say, I wrote off everything I was supposed to do and hauled books off my special shelves.

In one volume, the text described the spider's position as arch-trickster of the insect world, which we already knew. My next effort brought forth wonders.

The web, it was pointed out, is a spiral converging towards a central spot. It hardly needs pointing out that this describes a labyrinth. It also describes the gorgeous shells known as chambered nautilis which we gave one another for Christmas after our initial labyrinth adventure.

The spider in its web, continues the article (written by our old friend Cirlot), is a symbol of the center of the world.

> Spiders, in their ceaseless weaving and killing—building and destroying—symbolize the ceaseless alternation of forces on which the stability of the universe depends. The symbolism of the spider goes deep, signifying...man's continual transmutation throughout the course of his life. Even death itself merely winds up the thread of an old life in order to spin a new one.

A third book relates that a single spider thread can be climbed to and from the heavens (by whom and when we are not told) and also that the entire web can on occasion serve as a basket to carry souls to the next world.

Arch-trickster, hub of the world, psychopomp and symbol of eternity! Have we ever been presented with anything quite so momentous, so—well breathtaking?

Before I could properly digest any of this we had to go out to dinner. I wore my best black slacks. Arrived at our destination, I hung up my coat, strolled into the living room and sat down. Instantly, a spider appeared on my lap, ran down my pant leg and vanished under the sofa.

Despite the fact that I knew Sandy was up to her ears with guests, I called her with the above information. Although suitably overcome, she went right to what is probably the heart of the matter.

"It's the same old thing," she said. "He doesn't want us to finish the book. The nearer we get, the more stunning the effort, but he forgets that we're prisoners of time. He isn't."

SANDY

And that's not all. After Rusty's call I had a sudden memory.

We were having lunch in a restaurant on the top floor of a very high building. It was late fall and the air was cold. So was the room which had one whole wall of wide, floor length windows. Our table was just in front of one of these windows and we saw to our amazement that on the outside the entire width at the top was covered with a fringe of black spiders. We have always been intrigued with spiders and their accomplishments and way of life but never had we even read of anything like this.

I called Rusty right back and she vividly remembered everything. Neither of us, however, could dig up a single memory as to where or when this experience took place or how we could have forgotten it for so many years. I guess we had simply let a Hermes clue slide by us, so it must have happened early in the game. It returned, as you will now hear, with a vengeance.

When these spiders and spider memories appeared, we were all set to go on a trip. Coincidence? Certainly not. We deal with contingency, not coincidence.

RUSTY

We met in Savannah, Sandy's time being too full and health (for the moment) too frail to travel any further. We went of course to our same beloved inn and the same beloved blue room.

We were only half unpacked when she said, "I can't wait any longer. I've got to tell you right now."

Apparently, she was standing under a tree on her island, talking with a friend when suddenly something fell on her shoulder. Her friend reached for it, but it scuttled across the back of her shoulders and reappeared on her other side. Another grab sent it racing across her collar bone to the original shoulder. The hunt, finally succeeding, revealed a brown and greenish creature about three inches long, identified by Sandy's friend as a praying mantis.

The persistence of this personage, much like that of the spider, persuaded us that insect was probably our hermetic clue.

Off we waltzed to the nearest bookstore, but found only what we already knew—that the praying mantis, clasping his forelegs beneath his chin, resembles someone deep in prayer, and also that the female is unfortunately inclined to eat her mate if he isn't bright enough to flee after performing his marital duty. Just before guiltily returning the book to its shelf unbought, we read that the praying mantis is the single insect who can look over his or her shoulder—not perhaps of vital importance but definitely a hermetic touch.

Incidentally, you can identify this party by dropping the word praying, but in that case you have to say mantid, not mantis. Why? Ask your nearest entomologist. It always intrigues me to come upon the idiosyncrasies of scientists. I'm not the only one who's quirky.

So where were we? Obviously on a paper chase—and probably a very sly and complex one. We returned to our B & B to ponder.

Maybe the arachnid in the bathtub, a fellow Chief Trickster after all, was just a way for H. to say, "Here I am." Or maybe the whole spider thing was a prelude to lure our attention to the p.m.? After much cogitation, we gave a yes to both propositions.

If this sounds not only unlikely but crazy, you have to realize, Melanie, that we are speaking and hearing a language that we've been learning for more than 60 years. If you tuned in to a chat between Bushmen, it would sound insane—but it works for them. The language that H. has taught us works for us and him.

All right. So Hermes is very much here and the mantid is important. Now what?

We never try to decipher a whole pageant in a day. It tends to take up the exact amount of time we have—five days in this case—so we dropped our pursuit for the moment and went to work reviewing all the bad stuff that had occurred since last we met—our horrors, as Sandy always calls them, that have to be cleared out of the way of the good stuff. After that we make our first move. We used to think it was an independent move, but now we know who's behind things.

Sandy suggested that just for old time's sake we go up to the out-of-this-world attic where we worked the last time we stayed here. Up we went.

On the door of the bathroom which Clementine had described as haunted was a sign: KNOCK BEFORE ENTERING.

That 999 bathroom doors out of any 1,000 guarantee privacy with a lock instead of a sign made us cackle with glee. It is always the thousandth case that assures us who is present.

On a table outside the bathroom door was a bowl. It was for sale for $15. Who—and where—were the customers? Clearly another clue had appeared. We studied the bowl,and we were charmed, captivated and finally captured for good and all.

The whole inside depicted a scene which could possibly tell a story—if we knew who the characters might be. That they were all men was neither here nor there. What staggered us was their occidental faces, bright red hair and clearly Chinese clothes, horses and general ambiance! There was a crowned king, first at a dinner party and then in a boat with his courtiers. The boat had a wildly decorated hull, the main motif being horseshoes, a shower curtain for a mainsail, a bath towel for a topsail and an umbrella for a jib. All the passengers were looking intently in one direction. In the opposite direction was a young horseman, perhaps a prince, waving wildly.

Fascinating little bits of froth were scattered about, serving as both clouds and waves. What was sea and what was air was left up to you. Dwellings were flung about, above and below the sea—oriental, occidental and never-never-landish, some upright, some tilted, all brilliantly colored. A blacksmith on the outside of the bowl practiced his craft in front of a gaudy palace while a character carrying an axe and a pair of clippers capered in front of what might have been a theater, a temple or a dream not quite finished. We had to have the bowl and we had to have it right now.

There ensued a series of intricate scenes, the kind to which we have been long accustomed, but which are wearying to the aged. The bowl's label with the $15 price also gave the name of an antique emporium in a very chic part of town. We found it, found that an old friend of Sandy's was now owner and found out how the bowl got to the magic attic.

"We supervised an estate sale up there some time ago. None of the things were ours, but I remember that Chinese bowl. Nobody wanted it and it has little value so we just left it. It's never been claimed."

"But we want it desperately," we wailed. "How can we get it?"

"I'll have to think about it," said Sandy's friend.

We went for a walk through Savannah's inviting garden squares and briefly listened to a West Point band. (No, I don't know why it was there. It's just the kind of thing that shows up on our trips.) Finally we returned to our home-away-from-home for a cup of tea.

On the concierge's desk was a parcel from the antique shop.

The next morning Sandy phoned our ecstatic thanks. She did not ask any direct Chinese bowl questions, but she did inquire as to who might be able to explain its strangeness.

"My Uncle Arthur," was the reply.

Uncle Arthur was also an antiquarian and we wandered off, bowl in hand, to another emporium of gorgeous antiquities. Arthur was not expected, however, for at least an hour, so off we went to a lunch spot warmly recommended by one of Uncle Arthur's assistants. It didn't look like much from the outside—or the inside either. Our eyes swept to the right and then to the left—and then stopped.

On the cashier's counter was a brochure telling of a special exhibit at a Savannah art institute. A prize was to be given to what a panel of judges considered the best design for a new Hermes scarf! The brochure showed several designs, the most striking of course on the cover—exactly where we would have put it. We sat down and ordered soup, but what we gobbled up was the brochure.

All Hermes scarves, we read, were made of purest silk from China. The cover design was of Chinese figures dressed like those on our bowl, riding cavorting steeds through little bits of froth that might or might not have been waves.

We more or less floated back to Uncle Arthur's gallery. Charming he most certainly turned out to be, with an enticing old world courtesy and something else which slowly took over. This, more or less, is what he said:

"I have to tell you that this is a modern piece, made in China for the export trade and of little financial value." A long pause ensued and I asked quaveringly whether it told a story. He did not answer and Sandy and I both reached for the bowl. He held on.

"It's interesting. It's a wild, exuberant piece of work." Pause. Smile. "You keep seeing something new, don't you?"

Pause. "Don't try to make it tell any story. It will tell you what it wants to. You'll find something new in it forever."

Uncle Arthur stood up. We stood up. With great tenderness he handed us the bowl. "This," he said, "is a treasure."

We wandered homeward, taking turns carrying our precious hermaion, but suddenly Sandy grabbed my arm. "What about the mantid?" she cried.

We stopped dead, our exuberance fading.

"All right," I moaned, "but it's awfully late to go way out to the library."

"Let's try the bookstore once more," Sandy insisted. "There must be an insect book we missed."

And of course there was—a slim little book crouching almost unseen among the large aggressive volumes. There wasn't much about the mantid, but there was enough.

"It comes," we read, "from China."

"So now," I quavered, "we do what?"

SANDY

I am beginning to suspect that this wondrous, joyous, glorious revelation is going to prove endless – a forever kind of thing. Every time we decide to write The End, we have to erase it.

Something very strange has now happened and obviously, as always, has to be contemplated. Jim, a young friend who has been reading our manuscript, just called.

"Around ten o'clock last night," he said, "I turned the last page and was headed for bed. Instead, however, I found that I had to go out, get in my truck and drive through the woods. As if under orders, I suddenly stopped, dismounted and walked along the riverbank, arriving at a large, ancient oak, leaning way out over the water. On the trunk lay an iron shape. I picked it up and, in the moonlight, saw that it was a hinge. I also saw that it was both rusty and sandy."

RUSTY

A few days later, my daughter Felicity phoned. She was, she said, giving her significant other a goose for his birthday and suddenly realized she didn't know anything about geese. The birthday party was about to begin.

"You've got animal books in your own library," I suggested.

"No, no, no" she panted impatiently. "I want to know about spiritual, mystical, legendary geese, the kind of information that is in your library."

"I'll call you back" I suggested, but there was apparently no time. She had to know NOW. I picked out one of the fattest, most reliable of my mythological volumes and read to her.

"The expression 'silly goose' is of pious derivation, the word silly originally meaning blessed." The goose, it seems, was not only long considered a blessed fowl (like the swan and the crane) but a very special "bird of heaven" to boot. Brahma himself had a chariot drawn by a goose "as swift as thought" and in medieval times geese were believed to be familiars to witches, serving them as steeds.

The word goose in certain ancient tongues means "great light." Moreover, "in many languages, the name for goose also means sun."

And here we go – hardly, by this time unexpectedly. Goose flesh had already begun to erupt: "The goose is sacred to Apollo, Dionysus, Hermes and Thoth."

Of course, I called Sandy right off and of course we both sang the old litany: "Is anyone likely to believe any of this? Probably not, but it happened."

The happening, however was not finished. "Why" wailed Sandy, "was she giving her significant other a goose? And what kind of goose? Alive? Stuffed? Porcelain? Marble?"

Well, the recipient lives in a condo, so a live personage could be promptly ruled out. As to the other possibilities, I was in the dark. It should go without saying that I phoned my daughter the next morning.

"Just have to know" I ventured, "why you decided on a goose for a birthday present."

"I didn't," came the reply.

She continued: "I went to a gift shop to buy a pair of candlesticks. The woman in charge said that some new, very nice ones were in the store room—newly arrived. I found them, liked them and carried them back into the shop. The owner was now standing just inside the door clutching an absolutely gorgeous stuffed goose. 'I don't know what to do with this,' she said. 'There's just this one and it doesn't fit in with anything else.' I asked her if I could buy it."

"Of course," the owner said to Felicity. So of course she did.

"But does he like geese?" I enquired, totally enthralled and recognizing the touch.

"I don't think so – well really I don't know. I just had to buy that goose. It's sort of hard to explain."

It is indeed. Indeed it is.

Just before bedtime, I decided to glance through one of what I think of as my second-best reference volumes.

"Geese," I read, "are messengers from the spirit world."

SANDY

This is it – definitely and conclusively, the last blast we can cope with. We're TOO OLD.

Three years ago, in one night, all my beloved geese disappeared. There was no sign of a struggle and not one feather was found. Of course we searched everywhere, but the mystery was never solved. One of the geese, whose name was Christmas, loved me dearly, followed me everywhere and ate out of my hand. I was devastated.

Now, three weeks ago I was swinging and reading just outside my house when I heard a call. I looked around and there, without any question, was Christmas—fit, strong and apparently unchanged. He hopped right up to me and took a cracker from my hand. Now he announces himself every morning beneath my window, shouting for his cracker—and hangs around the horses just as he used to. He had been gone for three years.

RUSTY

As always, there we are, struck amidship. What is there new to say?

And then, abruptly, I realized that this time, however late

the date, there was something new to ponder:

Hermes has never brought even one outsider into the story, never mind two! The arrival on the scene of Jim and Felicity is pretty stunning. Is Hermes planning to enlarge the cast, intensifying the dramatic complexities? If so, how can two nonegenarions possibly bear up? Only one of Us Three is immortal. Only one is tireless.

And what can we possibly do about it? Nothing.

SANDY and RUSTY

We no longer feel that we can ever authoritatively write FINIS to this tale, nor can we risk TO BE CONTINUED, because, as always, we don't know.

But both of us want to offer a few summing up thoughts – not just for you, Melanie, but for all the grands and greats present and the great-greats to come.

Listen to Campbell: "Every hero whether ancient or new, begins by separating himself from what he has known, whether it be his kingdom or his tea cups. He does so in answer to some call to adventure from a mysterious source that reverberates throughout his being. Consciousness is newly awakened, anything seems possible."

Your grandmother and your great aunt may not look like heroes, ancient or new, but that is exactly what has happened to us—so remember this:

Don't ever, ever think four dimensions, five senses and the human intellect are the only paths to truth. And don't let any scientist, no matter what his discipline, nor any priest, no matter what his theology, push you around. Hear them, by all means, but keep a secret space inviolable—swept and bright—and be very sure that the doors and windows are always open as wide as they will go.

SANDY

It is impossible to believe what happened just now. I was walking…

Permissions

Excerpts from MASKS OF GOD: OCCIDENTAL MYTHOLOGY by Joseph Campbell, copyright (c) by Joseph Campbell. Used by permission of Viking Penguin, a division of Penguin Group (USA) Inc.

Excerpts from ANGELS: AN ENDANGERED SPECIES by Malcolm Godwin (copyright 1990) reprinted by permission of RLR Associates.

Excerpts from TRICKSTER MAKES THIS WORLD: MISCHIEF, MYTH AND ART by Lewis Hyde. Copyright (c) 1998 by Lewis Hyde. Reprinted by permission of Farrar, Straus and Giroux, LLC.

Excerpts from HERMES, GUIDE OF SOULS by Karl Kerenyi (copyright 1987) reprinted by permission of Spring Publications, Inc.

"Behold a Pale Horse" by Elizabeth Pool reprinted by permission of Yankee Publishing, Inc., as printed in *Yankee Magazine*, December 1997.

Excerpts from A LIFE OF PICASSO by John Richardson (copyright 1991) reprinted by permission of Random House, Inc.

Excerpts from THE GODS OF GREECE by Arianna Stassinopoulos Huffington (copyright 1989) reprinted by permission of Harry N. Abrams, Inc.

Excerpts from MEN AND ANGELS by Theodora Ward (copyright 1969) reprinted by permission of McIntosh and Otis, Inc.

Excerpts from THE DANCING WU LI MASTERS: AN OVERVIEW OF THE NEW PHYSICS by Gary Zukav (copyright 1972) reprinted by permission of HarperCollins Publishers.

Elizabeth Pool graduated from a prep school in New York and was headed to Vassar, but she made a proposition to her father: Could she go to the Orient instead, spending four months in the Pacific and end up in Japan? In the early 1930s, this was no ordinary request, particularly with a proposed female companion. Her father, an Englishman, gave his consent, for he had spent his young adulthood as part of the British Raj in India, which persuaded him towards the education value of travel.

On her return, instead of entering Vasser, she got married. Over the ensuing years, she went through half a dozen colleges while also becoming a wife and mother.

Pool spent 16 years writing a three-volume world history of mankind, Prologue to the Present in the '80s. Other published works are Unicorn Was There and The Unexpected Messiah, both published in the '60s.

During the '40s, Pool became Vice President of the Board of Trustees of Bard College, which had just broken away from Columbia University. She also served as a delegate to the first convention of the National Association for the Repeal of Abortion Laws, Chicago, 1969, which initiated the landmark Supreme Court case Roe vs. Wade.

Through the years, Pool has been a lecturer, both paid and unpaid, on a variety of subjects. She likes to write, produce, design, and direct pageants.

Pool resides in Dublin, New Hampshire.

Eleanor West has participated in an assortment of preservation efforts, foundations and projects, as well as several creative endeavors. She organized the address for preserving wilderness on barrier islands, and appeared as a key speaker at the Marshlands Conference in 1968. She wrote, narrated and co-produced a film titled Search for Ecological Balance in cooperation with Dr. Eugene P. Odum on the subject of the preservation of the coastal area.. She also conveyed Ossabaw Island to the State of Georgia, making Ossabaw Island the first Heritage Preserve property under Georgia's Heritage Trust Program.

West helped to create The Ossabaw Island Foundation, which oversees and operates the programs which bring thousand of people to the Island to study, pursue projects and learn; The Ossabaw Island Project, which allowed people of creative purpose in all disciplines to pursue their work at Ossabaw; The Genesis Project, which enabled qualified people to carry out projects in the sciences, arts, and humanities; The Professional Research Program, where qualified scientists and students studied Ossabaw's environment and conducted non-disruptive experiments; and the Public Use and Education Program, which arranges week- or day-long visits to Ossabaw for the general public.

West assisted in the production of numerous films which highlight the sculpture and architecture of the Italian Renaissance, and also worked on the production of films on two contemporary artists, Harry Bertoia and Arnold Blanch. In addition, she authored two books for children, including Maria Bosomworth and William Rogers, which received the Award of Excellence from the 1976 Southern Books Competition.

West has served on the Board of Directors for the Franklin Settlement, the Boys Republic, the Roeper School for Gifted Children, and Brookside School Cranbrook in Bloomfield Hills, Michigan. She was a Chair for the American Red Cross Nurses Aides and the Detroit Chapter of Planned Parenthood.

West's many awards and recognitions include a Gold Metal from the Michigan Academy of Arts and Sciences for her contribution to the arts and the Georgia Trust for Historic Preservation in March 1995, recognizing her long-term stewardship of a historic property.

West resides on Ossabaw Island in Georgia.